DIXIE & STRIPES

GILBERT MORRIS

MOODY PRESS
CHICAGO

ISBN: 0-8024-3364-2

3 5 7 9 10 8 6 4 2

Printed in the United States of America

Everybody needs a best friend—and my best friend is Dixie Morris. From the time I first picked her up when she was only a few hours old, I said to myself, "This young lady and I are going to be the best friends in the whole world!"

Everybody says I'm just Dixie's big toy, that she plays with me as if I were just another one of her Barbie dolls—a big one! When she was nine I wrote the first of the Dixie Morris novels for her. It's taken a long time to get them published. Now she's a beautiful young lady of fifteen, but we're still best friends—and always will be!

Gilbert Morris

CONTENTS

1. A New Adventure   7
2. An Unhappy Girl   15
3. Here Comes the Parade!   31
4. Dixie Finds a Friend   49
5. Moving the Big Top   65
6. A Real Pussycat   73
7. Three Fine Babies   83
8. The Circus at Work   99
9. Dixie Goes to Church   117
10. Terror Under the Big Top   127
11. The Matchmaker   139
12. A Tiger in the Dark   151
13. Dolls Aren't So Bad   163

Aunt Sarah, I want to stop at the next Taco Bell we come to. I'm starving!"

Sarah Logan took her eyes off the twisting road just long enough to glance at her ten-year-old niece, Dixie. "No, we stopped at Taco Bell yesterday at noon. Today it's my turn. I want some Chinese food."

The two were sitting in the front seat of a red Dodge pickup, pulling a silver Airstream trailer. They were in the mountains of Tennessee, headed for Chattanooga, and it took nearly all of Aunt Sarah's concentration to keep the big truck and trailer on the road.

"I'll compromise with you, Dixie," she said with a smile. "We'll stop at Taco Bell for lunch, but tonight we find a Chinese restaurant, all right?"

"All right, Aunt Sarah." Dixie patted her aunt's hand. She thought that Aunt Sarah was the best-looking woman in the world—for an older woman.

Sarah Logan had bright red hair and green eyes. Her hands were strong and capable, which was good, because she was a veterinarian and needed strength to handle the animals that came under her care. Now she glanced at Dixie again. "You're going to wear out that doll if you don't give her a rest."

"No, I won't." Dixie held up a Barbie doll. It was only one of her large collection of Barbies. She smoothed the doll's hair, saying, "This is my favorite, Aunt Sarah. She was my very first Barbie."

"She looks like all the rest of them to me."

"Aunt Sarah, don't say that! They're all different!"

"When I was a girl, we had chubby dolls that looked like real babies." She looked over at the doll and frowned. "I'm not sure it's good for you to play with those things all the time."

"Why not?" Dixie asked. "What's wrong with Barbies?"

"They may give you a wrong idea about

what women are supposed to look like. I don't know any women who are as perfect as a Barbie doll."

"Oh, I know that."

Dixie played with her dolls until she spotted a Taco Bell. She had two soft tacos, and Aunt Sarah ate a taco salad. Then they got back into the truck and continued their trip.

At four o'clock Aunt Sarah pulled the rig into a campground and breathed a sigh of relief. "Well, let's get set for the night, then we'll go find some food."

Sarah received their location from the attendant. She backed the trailer into the space and released the trailer from the truck. Dixie helped her make the hookups that provided water and sewage and lights for the trailer. Then she said, "I'm hungry again, Aunt Sarah."

Thirty minutes later they were sitting in the Crimson Dragon, a small restaurant that Aunt Sarah had spotted before they had parked. Dixie was eating with such enthusiasm that her aunt said, "I thought you didn't like Chinese food."

"It's all right—if you can't get Mexican food."

When the waitress brought them some ice cream, Aunt Sarah said, "We'll get to Chattanooga some time tomorrow, Dixie. Are you excited about joining the Royal Circus?"

"I sure am. I think it's going to be more fun than anything."

Dixie's parents were in Africa as short-term missionaries. Before coming to live with Aunt Sarah, she had stayed on a farm with other relatives for several months. Recently her father wrote, saying:

> Dixie, it's still too rough for children in this place, but as soon as possible we'll try to fix up a nice home. Then you can come and be with us. For now, I know you'll enjoy your time with Aunt Sarah, and we're praying that God will keep you.

"Do you miss your parents?" Sarah asked gently.

"Oh, sure." Dixie nodded. "But I understand how it is. The last letter I got, Mama said there wasn't even a bathroom in the house. And the mosquitoes are terrible. I know I'm better off here." She looked up, smiling. "It's going to be fun at the circus. And I don't have to worry about school for three months!"

Sarah laughed a tinkling sound. "I think you'll like the circus, and you've gotten some experience already, working with Jumbo."

"I sure do miss him." Dixie sighed, thinking of the elephant that she had helped save from being "put down," which meant being put to death.

"Well," Sarah said, "they'll have lots of elephants in the circus. I'm sure you'll make friends with many of them."

It was dark when they went back to the trailer. She loved the Airstream. It was not large, but it had everything, including a small kitchen and a bathroom with a shower and tub. For eating, there was a table that folded down and could be made into a bed in case of company.

Dixie's own special place was the bed next to the back of the trailer. Aunt Sarah had fitted that area with cabinets so that she could keep all her dolls there, as well as shoes and clothes. Now, as it was still early, she lined up all her dolls and repeated their names.

Aunt Sarah stuck her head in. "It's time for your shower and then to bed."

Dixie put her dolls away and grabbed her pj's. When she was ready for bed, her aunt sat beside her and read a psalm from the Bible. Then she took Dixie's hand. "I'm glad you're with me, sweetheart," she said. "Let's pray that God will keep us safe, and that He will use us as we join the circus."

They both prayed. Then Aunt Sarah pulled the cover over Dixie and kissed her. "Sleep tight. Tomorrow's a big day."

Dixie was tired. She clutched her favorite Barbie and whispered, "Tomorrow we'll be circus people. Won't that be fun, Celeste?"

2
AN
UNHAPPY GIRL

O h, Chattanooga's so pretty!"
Dixie looked out the truck window,
craning her neck to see the mountains that
rose sharply over the city. The sun was set-
ting, throwing crimson rays on the under-
side of the clouds.

"That's Lookout Mountain over there,"
Aunt Sarah said. "One of the great battles
of the Civil War was fought there."

"Maybe we can go see the battlefield,"
Dixie said hopefully.

"Perhaps, but the circus doesn't stay
very long in one place."

They stopped at a convenience store
for gas. As Sarah paid, she asked, "Do you
know where the circus is located?"

"Yes, ma'am." The thin young man
who handed over her change pointed. "You

take this street right here until you head out of town. It's in a big field out there." He glanced out at the Airstream and asked eagerly, "Are you one of the performers?"

"No, I'm just going to take care of the animals. Thank you so much."

The traffic was not heavy, so both Dixie and her aunt could enjoy looking at the city as they drove through it. Then Dixie saw a big tent in the middle of a field. "There it is!" she cried. "There's the circus!"

Ahead was the circus Big Top. Cars were already parked in the huge pasture, and the sound of a calliope came across the early evening air.

"I believe we're just in time for the show." Sarah turned in, her eyes searching the lot. "See those trailers? I bet that's where the circus people live." She drove the Airstream to the section where trailers and campers of all sorts were scattered over the green grass. She turned off the engine, and they got out.

Sarah stopped a very large man and said, "Excuse me, I'm looking for a place to put my trailer."

The big man was joined suddenly by a boy about ten. He had the same blond hair as the man. "Hi," he said to Dixie. "What's your name?"

"Dixie Morris."

"I'm Eric Von Bulow." He glanced at the Airstream. "Are you going to be with the circus?"

"I'm the new veterinarian," Aunt Sarah said. "My name is Sarah Logan."

"Ah—I am Karl Von Bulow," the man said. "You have heard of me, no doubt."

"Uh . . . I'm not sure," Sarah said. "You're with the circus, then?"

"Certainly! Von Bulow's Stallions." He folded his arms over his massive chest. "You don't know much about the Royal Circus, do you?"

"Not a great deal yet." Sarah smiled apologetically. "I just got out of veterinarian college. But I'm sure I will."

"My horses demand much care!" Von Bulow said sternly. "When will you be coming by to check on them?"

"Oh, as soon as I can get settled in. Could you tell me who to talk to about putting my trailer in the right place?"

"I'll show them," Eric said. He walked over to Dixie. "How old are you?"

"I'm ten. How old are you?"

"I'm ten too. When is your birthday?"

"July the third."

"Then I'm three months older than you are, so you have to do what I say." He laughed and grabbed her firmly by the arm. "Come on, I'll take you to Mr. Bennigen."

Eric towed Dixie along. She didn't like being pulled as if she were a wagon, and she decided she didn't like Eric Von Bulow very much.

Then she saw a short thin man with red hair and blue eyes, approaching at a half run.

"Hey, Ace! Here's the new vet!"

The man stopped and glared at Eric. "I told you! When you get to be eighteen, you can call me Ace. Until then, I'm Mr. Bennigen."

"Sure, Mr. Bennigen," Eric said cheerfully. "This is Sarah Logan, and this is Dixie Morris. Sarah's the new vet."

Bennigen pulled off his soft felt hat. "Well, I'm glad to see you, Dr. Logan. I'm the circus manager. We've got several animals that need some care."

"If you'll show me where to park my trailer . . ."

"Right this way. I saved a good slot for you. We've been expecting you."

All the time that Sarah was backing the trailer into her parking place, Eric was pestering Dixie with questions.

Finally she said, "Look, Eric, I'm going to be with the circus from now on. I'll be glad to tell you everything you want to know but not right now!"

"Well, ain't you a stuck-up one!" Eric said indignantly. He punched her in the stomach so hard that it took her breath away. Then he ran off, laughing. "See you later," he called back.

"Don't pay any attention to that brat," Ace Bennigen said. "He's a pain in the neck." Then he turned to Sarah. "I hate to put you to work right away, but we've got a problem."

"What is it, Mr. Bennigen?"

"Oh, you can just call me Ace. It's one of Delaney's tigers. Something's wrong with him. How about we go take a look right now?"

"That'll be fine."

Dixie's eyes were wide. Everything was exciting. A small carnival had evidently joined up with the circus.

"They're not part of the show," Mr. Bennigen said. "But carnivals like to latch onto us. You like carnival rides?"

"Oh yes!"

"Well, you can ride free all you want to. Just let them know that you're with the circus." Then he nodded at a smaller tent that was connected to the Big Top. "Here's the menagerie. Come on in."

The menagerie tent was filled with animals of all sorts, including horses, dogs, and three bears that were being groomed. But Bennigen went by all of these to where a tall man, a girl, and a woman stood talking.

"This is Val Delaney. The Great Delaney, as he likes to call himself."

Val Delaney gave the manager an irritated look. "I never call myself that!" He wore a pair of white jodphurs, and his white shirt was embroidered with gold braid. His black boots came up over his calves, and Dixie thought he was as handsome as Tom Cruise!

"This is Dr. Sarah Logan, our new vet."

"Glad to know you, Dr. Logan. Oh, and this is Helen Langley."

"How are you, Sarah?" Helen said. She had green eyes and a wealth of brown hair.

"Are you one of the performers, Helen?" Sarah asked.

"Oh no. I'm just a lowly accountant."

"Don't you believe it," Bennigen said. He grinned at the woman. "Her title is assistant manager, and she does most of the things that I can't get to around here."

Val Delaney said, "And this is my daughter, Lindsey."

"Hello," the girl said cautiously. She had brown hair with red lights in it, large brown eyes, and was very pretty. She was about Dixie's age. Finally, Lindsey said, "I'm glad you've come to be with the circus, Dixie."

"Thank you. I don't know much about circuses yet."

Val Delaney cut this conversation short by saying, "I've got a real problem with Stripes—"

A dog suddenly came up, rubbed against Helen Langley's legs, and began barking loudly.

"Be quiet, Tater!" she said, bending over to pet him.

Dixie admired the dog. "What kind is that?"

"He's what's called a Red Walker hound."

"Look, we don't have much time," Val

said. "I've got to go on in a few minutes. There's the cue for the Von Bulows." He appraised Sarah with some doubt and said, "I'm sorry, but . . . well, you're very young. Have you had any experience with tigers?"

"No, I haven't," Sarah admitted, "but they're big cats, and I've had a lot of experience with cats."

"They're not nice like cats!" Lindsey snapped. "They're hateful and mean!"

A glance passed between Val Delaney and Helen Langley, and the tall man said, "They make a living for us, Lindsey. Come along, Dr. Logan. I'll give you a quick look at your patient."

Dixie stayed close to the adults as they passed a row of cages filled with tigers. Several growled at them. Then they reached a cage that held an enormous tiger.

"This is a Siberian tiger," Val Delaney said. "The farther north tigers live, the bigger they grow. Isn't he a beauty?"

Dixie moved closer to the cage and stared at the magnificent beast on the inside. His eyes were on them. And then he opened his tremendous mouth and emitted a roar so loud that she jumped back against Sarah.

"What seems to be the trouble with him, Mr. Delaney?"

"Just call me Val. We don't go much for 'misters' around the circus. And I don't know what's the matter with him."

Lindsey said, "You ought to get rid of him, Daddy. I hate him."

Aunt Sarah gave the girl a surprised look. She did not ask any questions, however, but said, "You may have to help me a little bit, Val, since I haven't been around big cats like this."

"Well, it's too late to do anything right now, Doctor—or can I call you Sarah?"

"Of course. When could I examine him?"

"After the performance. We'll get his nerves all calmed down, and then maybe you can check him over." He ran a hand through his hair. "I had great hopes for him. His mother, Sultana, was the best tiger I ever had. I'd hoped Stripes would be like her."

"What happened to her?"

"She died just a few months ago—there's my cue." He grabbed up a small baton lying by the cage and left, calling to a young man who suddenly appeared, "Kirk, there's the cue! It's time for the act!"

"Come on, Dixie," Lindsey said abruptly. "I'll take you around and introduce you to some of the other people."

"I'd like to see the tiger act."

"Oh, all right, but you'll be seeing it a lot."

Dixie watched the Great Delaney. He did not carry a whip, as she had expected, but only the small baton. As the tigers entered the cage, he had each jump up on a perch until they all circled him. Dixie was thrilled to see him in the cage with eight full-grown tigers.

She noticed that all of them seemed well behaved—except for Stripes. Once he simply refused to get off of his stool no matter how much the Great Delaney urged him. When the act was over, he did come off but made a short run at the trainer. Val shouted in his face and slapped him on the nose with the baton.

Dixie was frightened, for the huge tiger was obviously stronger than any man, and the baton was no weapon at all. She took a deep breath as Stripes finally began slinking toward the exit of the big cage. "That scares me to death."

Lindsey looked at her. "It scares me

too. I wish Daddy did something else—anything but get in with those tigers! The Marinos are next. Do you like to watch fliers?"

"What are fliers?"

Lindsey pointed upward to where the lights were focused on the trapeze act.

Dixie was thrilled again, watching the trim fliers flip through the air to be caught by the catcher. "Don't you just love the circus?"

"I hate it!" Lindsey's face was twisted with anger, and her eyes were bitter. "Every morning you get up in a different place. You never get to know anybody. I want to live in a white house with a backyard and be at the same place all the time. I want a regular home." She turned and ran away.

Dixie thought she'd seen tears in the girl's eyes, and she felt sorry for her.

"Hey, there! What's *your* name?"

Dixie stopped at the sound of somebody's deep voice. She turned, expecting to see a big man, but instead she looked into the eyes of a man shorter than herself.

"I'm Bigg!"

"You are?"

"I don't mean I'm big, tall, or heavy. I mean that's my name, Bigg. B–I–G–G."

The speaker was obviously a full-grown man, but he was little more than two-and-a-half feet tall. He was looking up at Dixie, and his brown eyes twinkled merrily. "My name is Russell Hamilton Bigg, but everybody just calls me Bigg."

"I'm glad to know you, Mr. Bigg."

"Not 'mister.' Just Bigg." The dwarf put out his hand and gave Dixie's a hearty shake. "I saw you come in with your mother."

"No, that's my aunt. She's the new veterinarian."

"So you're new to the circus, then."

"Yes. I've always loved circuses, and now, for a while, I'll be here all the time."

"That's good. Maybe I can teach you to do some clown work."

"Oh, I could never do that!"

"Never can tell. I never thought I'd be a clown either, but I like it better than anything," Bigg said. "Come on, and I'll show you around."

As they walked about the grounds, Bigg pointed out the performers.

Then Dixie asked, "What's wrong with Lindsey? She seems real unhappy."

Bigg stopped abruptly.

It seemed strange to Dixie to be looking down at an adult. Bigg was wearing a tuxedo, which he had explained was part of one of his roles as a clown. She said, "What about her mother? I didn't meet her."

Bigg shuffled his feet and pulled his top hat off his head. "That's a sad story," he said. "Her mother died last year."

"Oh, that's too bad!" Dixie cried.

"Yes, it was. She was a performer with her husband. It was an unusual thing. Both of them were in the tiger cage—the rubes liked that."

"Rubes? What are rubes?"

"Aw, that's what we circus people call the people who watch the circus. We don't mean anything bad by it. Anyway, it was over a year ago now that Rita had an accident with the cats."

Suddenly Dixie thought she knew something. "Was it Sultana?"

"How did you know that?"

"Because Lindsey hates Stripes so much, and Sultana was Stripes's mother, isn't that right?"

"You're a smart cookie!" Bigg exclaimed. "That's right. She hates that big cat all right, which is a shame, because her dad likes him better than any of the rest of his tigers." He ran his hand over his bushy black hair and said sadly, "She's a sweet girl, Lindsey, but she hates the circus."

"Yes, she told me."

Bigg suddenly said, "I got to go. There's the sign for the final parade. But I'll be seeing you around, Dixie."

Dixie watched the small man run off, and she knew she had found a friend. But she could not help thinking of the pain in Lindsey Delaney's eyes and determined to make a friend of her too—if she could.

3

HERE COMES THE PARADE!

I just don't understand it," Sarah muttered. She threw herself into a chair. "That ought to be the healthiest tiger in the world."

Dixie had been sitting on her bed with her Barbie dolls spread out around her when her aunt came in. "How do you examine a tiger?" she asked. "Do you have to get in the cage with him?"

"No, Val got in the cage with him and got him to lie down close to the bars. I could take his temperature and check his pulse and do what I needed to do by reaching through the bars."

"I think he's so beautiful!"

"So do I, but he's not feeling well. His stomach was rumbling in a strange way, but I just couldn't figure it out."

"Where are we going to eat supper tonight? *My* stomach is rumbling."

"We'll go to the dining tent. We'll get to meet more of the performers that way. Are you ready?"

"No, I can't go like this!" Dixie was wearing a pair of cutoffs and a white T-shirt with a large green iguana on the front.

"I think you look fine."

Dixie merely sniffed and immediately began changing clothes. She put on a pair of new jeans and a lime-green blouse. Quickly she slipped her feet into matching green Keds, then went to the mirror and brushed her hair. "Aunt Sarah, when can I start wearing makeup?"

"When you're a little older than you are now," Sarah said. "Now, let's go."

The dining tent was just a short way from the Big Top. As they got closer, Dixie could smell food cooking, and when they stepped inside she saw long tables. Most of the chairs were already filled.

"Oh, here you are!" Bigg came running up and took Dixie's hand. "Come and sit with a gentleman, honey. You too, Doc."

Everyone had already begun calling Sarah "Doc."

Bigg led them to a table that was only half filled. "I don't think you've met the Sullivans. Well, this is Mooey Sullivan. Mooey, this is Dixie Morris and her Aunt Sarah. You want to watch out for this big Irishman. He's a preacher as well as an elephant trainer."

"Oh, do you train elephants, Mr. Sullivan?"

"Sure do, Dixie," Sullivan said. He was a large man with sandy hair and merry bright eyes. "Some say I do that better than I preach, but you'll have to find out when you come to church. This is Mrs. Sullivan and my son, Mickey."

Mickey was about Dixie's age and had his father's sandy hair and blue eyes.

"Do you like elephants, Dixie?" he asked.

"Oh, I love them!"

"She's quite an expert," Aunt Sarah said.

They sat down, and Bigg promptly filled Sarah's plate with a slice of roast beef, a big dollop of mashed potatoes and gravy, and a heaping spoonful of peas.

"Save room for dessert," he said.

"How did you get to be an expert on elephants?" Mickey asked.

He was a rather nice-looking boy, Dixie thought.

"Oh, I got to know one just this summer," she said.

Mickey listened as Dixie related how she and Chad Taylor had saved Jumbo from being put down. Then he smiled warmly. "I think that's the max! Not many girls would have the nerve to do a thing like that."

Dixie found herself talking freely with Mickey. He was one of those boys who were easy to know, and soon he was telling her about his life in the circus as Dixie cleaned her plate.

Dessert was pie—apple, cherry, and peach. Sarah said, "This is wonderful! I need to tell the cook."

"Well, there she is," Mooey Sullivan said. "Hey, Clara, come over here."

A big woman wearing a white apron was making her way among the tables. Her hair was rather wild, and when she said, "What do you want, Mooey?" her voice was the loudest in the tent.

"Clara, this is the new vet, Sarah Logan. And this is her niece, Dixie Morris. Clara Rendell is the most important person in the whole circus."

Sarah said quickly, "That's the best meal I've had in a long time, Clara. You're a wonderful cook. I wish you could teach me. I can't even boil water without burning it."

Clara laughed loudly. "I reckon I can do that." She looked at Dixie and said, "And you're old enough to learn. You come over sometime, and I'll show you how to make pie like this."

"I'll do that, Miss Clara," Dixie promised.

Ace Bennigen suddenly appeared at the table and grinned down at Dixie and Sarah. "All right. Time for you two to go to work."

"Is there a sick animal?" Sarah asked, starting to get up.

"There probably is, but that's not what I need you for. You two have got to help with the Grand Parade."

"You mean be *in* a parade?" Dixie asked.

"That's what I mean, sweetheart. We'll get you all dressed up."

"Dixie knows a lot about elephants. Could she ride on Ruth?" Mickey Sullivan piped up.

"I don't see why not, if she knows how. And we'll let you ride one of Von Bulow's

Stallions, Doc. Come on. Let's get your costumes."

Dixie and Sarah scrambled after Bennigen out of the dining tent and into a smaller one where a short, heavyset woman was almost surrounded by costumes.

"This is Dolly Stoltz. Here we go, Dolly! Two more volunteers for the Grand Parade—Doc Logan and Dixie Morris. Fix 'em up, will you?"

"All right, Ace." Dolly Stoltz looked at the two with a critical eye. "I think I'll let you be a harem girl, Dixie." She whirled about and opened a trunk. She leaned over it, and soon material was flying. Finally she brought out a filmy, rose-colored outfit. "Here, this was worn by one of the acrobats about your size. Go over behind that screen and put it on."

As Dixie left, Dolly said, "And I think we'll let you wear some spangles, Doc."

Dixie put on the costume. It was much like a swimsuit, and over it, covering her legs down to the ankles, was filmy, transparent material. There was a veil too. Then she came out from behind the screen, saying, "How do I look, Miss Dolly?"

"You look great, honey. Hurry up, Doc. The parade's about to start."

Slowly Sarah came out from behind her screen. She was wearing an outfit of light emerald green covered with spangles. "I can't wear this! It's too immodest!"

"That's what the fliers wear."

"Well, I'm not a flier! I'm a veterinarian!"

"You'll be wearing worse than this before long." Dolly grinned. "Under the Big Top we do what we got to do." She listened, then said, "There's the cue for the parade. Get going!"

Back at the menagerie tent, Dixie saw Mickey along with his parents and a line of elephants.

"Come over here, Dixie!" Mickey shouted. "You said you rode on an elephant?"

"Yes. I rode Jumbo. He was a lot bigger than this elephant."

"Then he was an African elephant. This is an Indian elephant. That's all we use in the circus. African elephants are too rambunctious. This elephant is Ruth." He tapped on Ruth's knee, and she laboriously knelt. "Can you get on by yourself?"

"Sure!" Dixie exclaimed. By pulling on Ruth's harness, she found herself straddling the animal's neck. "Up, Ruth!" she said, and the elephant heaved herself upright.

Mickey grinned up at her. "You're going to be great!"

Down the line behind the elephants, Aunt Sarah found Karl Von Bulow and his family, which included his wife, his son—Eric—and Marlene, Eric's twin. "Are you a rider?" Von Bulow asked.

"Well, I've been on a horse," Sarah said, "but not any as lively as these." She looked with apprehension at the tall gray stallions and swallowed hard. "I'll do the best I can."

"Oh, you'll be all right, Doc," Von Bulow said. "I trained these horses myself. You can ride Maxwell here." He indicated a gray stallion who looked at Sarah with a suspicious eye.

There were no saddles, and Sarah looked helplessly at the animal. "How do I get on?"

Von Bulow leaned over. "Put your foot in my hand." When it was there, he lifted her up as easily if she were made of air.

Sarah looked down nervously. "I don't know what to do," she said.

"You'll be third in line," Mrs. Von Bulow said. Then she turned to her husband. "You must be more considerate, Karl."

"Yes, dear." For all his size, Karl Von Bulow obeyed his wife docilely, which made Sarah smile.

In the big tent the Royal Circus band blared, and the flaps to the tent opened. Dixie felt Ruth stir under her, weaving back and forth, and then the line started up. Mickey's elephant was right behind hers. She looked around, and he grinned and waved.

As Ruth moved in under the Big Top, Dixie saw that the stands were full. She took it all in, the lights illuminating the trapeze overhead, the three rings where all the acts were done, the circle that went past the expensive seats and then to the cheaper ones. People waved. They called out to her, and she waved back.

The parade proceeded slowly around the ring while some of the acrobats turned back flips. From time to time Mooey Sullivan would call out a command, and all of the elephants would suddenly rear up. The first time that happened, Dixie was not ready, and she nearly fell off.

Eric Von Bulow was riding a horse right behind the elephants, and he yelled, "Hey, clumsy, you better get off and walk!"

Angry and embarrassed, Dixie grabbed Ruth's harness and determined to do better. The next time the command came, she was ready and held on with one hand, waving at the crowd with the other.

"That's the way to do it!" Mickey shouted.

When the parade was over, Dixie said, "Down!" and Ruth obediently knelt. She slipped to the ground and looked for Mickey. "That was fun!" she said.

"Well, I'm glad you liked it, because you'll be doing it a lot. Before every show and after."

All was confusion then, getting the animals back in place. She saw that Helen Langley, wearing a pair of jeans and a white blouse, was everywhere, helping Ace Bennigen move the acts into proper order.

Dixie found herself a place just inside the entrance and watched. She still got a catch in her throat every time Mia Marino and Brett Bailey, her partner, flew through the air to be caught by her father. Mr. Marino's wife could not fly any longer, Bigg had told her, but she kept the rhythm going by swinging the trapeze at just the right time.

"I wish I could do that," Dixie said aloud.

"It's too late for you, Dixie."

She turned around and saw a man who looked familiar.

He said, "I'm Kirk, Val's brother."

"Oh, how are you, Mr. Delaney?"

"Nobody calls me 'mister.' Just Kirk." Kirk was not as tall as his brother and was several years younger. He was wearing a disreputable pair of coveralls, which could stand washing. "You have to start when you're about three years old to learn to do that." He motioned upward to where Mia Marino performed a double somersault. The crowd exploded with applause. Dixie said, "She's so pretty."

"Sure is."

Something in Kirk Delaney's voice caught Dixie's attention. He was still watching the girl on the trapeze. He had not shaved for a day or two and would have been handsome, she thought, if he had combed his hair and taken better care of himself. Dixie wondered how he could be so different from Val.

"Well, there's the cue. Got to go help with the tiger act."

As he left, Bigg came over. "Too bad about him."

Dixie always felt it strange to find her eyes above those of an adult. "What's the matter with him, Bigg? Why doesn't he take a bath and shave?"

"He doesn't care about things like that."

"Why not?"

"It's a long story."

"Well, tell me," Dixie urged.

Bigg did not seem to want to gossip. "He used to be a fine young fellow, but he fell in love with the wrong girl. Another guy got her, and he hasn't been the same since."

"Oh, I know about things like that. When I see movies, I can always tell who's going to fall in love with who. I just know."

"Well, don't say anything about it. Keep your mouth shut, Dixie."

"Oh, I won't talk, except to you."

Bigg grinned. He had a wide mouth, and now that he was made up as a clown, it was even wider. He made a fine-looking clown with his red rubbery nose and the tuft of orange hair around what seemed to be a bald head. He reached up, pulled Dixie's hair, and said, "Got to go to work." He ran out under the lights and joined the other clowns, who were trying to put out a fire with buckets that had no water in them.

Dixie laughed at their antics.

And then it was time for the Great Delaney. She watched Kirk and some of the other roustabouts place a steel cage in the center ring. It was joined to a rectangular cage just the height of a tiger and just wide enough for the tigers to get in.

Val stepped into the cage, wearing his white costume with the gold braid, and smiled at the audience.

Dixie watched entranced as he put the huge cats through their paces. She noticed that Stripes was still hard to handle. Once, he made a swipe at Val, and Val smacked him on the nose with his baton.

The act ended to thunderous applause, and Dixie went out just in time to see the last of the tigers come through the chute into its cage. The cages were on wheels, and as soon as the tigers were in them, the doors were slammed shut.

Dixie looked up to see Val approaching, and his face was flushed with anger. "Kirk, what do you think you're doing?"

Kirk slammed the last door shut and said defiantly, "What are you talking about?"

"You nearly forgot to shut the door behind the cats! What if one of them had gotten loose?"

"I do my job," Kirk said sullenly.

"No, you don't! You don't do anything but loaf and stay drunk half the time! I'm telling you for the last time! You'd better straighten up, or you're out!"

Dixie saw the hurt that came into Kirk's eyes, but he did not answer.

Then she saw Lindsey standing over to one side. Once again Dixie noticed how unhappy the girl was. When the call came for the final parade, Dixie said, "Why don't you go get a costume, and we can do the parade together. It'd be fun!"

"No, I don't want to have anything to do with the circus." Lindsey walked away, leaving Dixie standing alone.

Suddenly something hit Dixie in the

back, knocking the breath out of her. She whirled angrily to see Eric Von Bulow.

"Hey, Dixie, go get on that big ugly elephant! If you really want to learn to ride something, I'll teach you how to ride a horse."

"I don't want to ride your old horse," Dixie cried, for his blow had hurt. She ran quickly to where the parade was forming.

Afterward, Dixie and Aunt Sarah walked back to their trailer. When Dixie had showered, she did not pick up her dolls as she usually did but sat down beside Sarah on the couch.

"I want to tell you something about the Delaneys," she said.

Sarah gave her a quick look. "Have you been meddling again, Dixie?"

"Me? I never meddle!"

"Never meddle? You never do anything else. But what about the Delaneys?"

Dixie ended her story by saying, "And so Kirk was in love with somebody, but she married somebody else. That made him so unhappy he started drinking, and now he's in love with Mia Marino, but she won't have anything to do with him because he drinks."

Aunt Sarah stared at Dixie and wagged her head in wonder. "How do you think up all these things?"

"But they're true!"

"Dixie, you're so used to making up stories about your dolls that you make up stories about real people. But people aren't Barbie dolls!"

"I know that," Dixie said indignantly, "but I guess I know what I see, don't I?"

"Well, you get into bed. After my shower we'll have our quiet time together, and we've got a busy day tomorrow. There are two shows, and I've got lots of animals to take care of."

Dixie went back to her bed and got into it. While Aunt Sarah sang in the shower, she thought about how her life had changed. She finally said aloud, "It sure is different living in a circus!"

4
DIXIE FINDS A FRIEND

There were so many things to be done at the circus and never enough help. Dixie found herself helping Dolly Stoltz, and she loved to work with the costumes. She tried on lots of them herself, even though most were too big.

One of her favorites was a costume that had been made for Mia Marino. Dixie pretended to be on the trapeze, flying through the air. She already had a crush on Brett Bailey, Mia's nineteen-year-old partner. Eric teased her unendingly about it. She had learned to ignore Eric, though, simply calling him a pain in the neck.

She also spent some time with Clara Rendell and learned to make biscuits. And she spent a lot of time with the Sullivans. She and Mickey had become good friends.

One day she said to him, "Elephants have to be awfully smart to dance in time to the music."

"They don't."

Dixie stared at him, puzzled. "Of course they do! I've seen them! Ruth can even do a hula dance."

"They can dance all right, but the music doesn't have anything to do with it."

They were in the trailer, playing Monopoly between shows, and Mickey had been enjoying the brownies and popcorn that Dixie had made. He explained, "You watch sometimes. The elephants dance, and then the band follows what *they* do—not the other way around."

"You're not teasing me, are you?"

"No. Really. That's the way it works. The band has to be pretty good to follow the dance of the elephants."

One morning at breakfast, Mickey said, "Well, we'll be leaving Chattanooga in two days."

"Where are we going?"

"Memphis."

"Have you been there before?"

"I suppose so." Mickey shrugged. "After you've been in the circus for a while, all places look about the same. Most of the time, all I see is the circus."

"Why, I think that's awful! Like, here in Chattanooga we could go to Lookout Mountain. I'll ask Aunt Sarah to take us."

As soon as breakfast was over, Dixie followed Sarah around as she examined the animals. "Aunt Sarah, could we have company for supper tonight?"

"Why? There's always dinner in the dining tent."

"I know, but everybody's been so nice to us. I thought we could fix supper for them. It'd be a treat. I'll help—I can cook pasta—and we could have brownies for dessert."

"Pasta and brownies!" Aunt Sarah smiled. "That wouldn't be much of a treat."

"I bet it would, and you could make some of that Chinese food you do so well."

She begged so hard that Sarah said, "Who did you want to ask?"

"Could we have the Sullivans and the Delaneys?"

"They'd fill up the trailer!"

"But they live in trailers, too!" Dixie said. "They know what it's like. Please, Aunt Sarah."

"Well, all right. You can ask them, but it would probably be better to ask them at different times."

Dixie, however, had a head full of schemes.

She went to invite the Sullivans. "Mickey," she said, finding her friend washing down the elephants with a garden hose, "Aunt Sarah said we could fix supper for you and your folks tonight—and for the Delaneys."

"Hey, that'd be great."

"Good. We're going to eat after the last performance. Now I've got to go ask the Delaneys."

Dixie's feet flew as she ran to Val's trailer.

Lindsey opened the door.

"Aunt Sarah says she wants you and your dad and Kirk to come to supper tonight."

"Oh. Well, I'll ask him." She called over her shoulder, "Dad, can we have supper with Sarah and Dixie tonight?"

Val Delaney suddenly appeared, wearing a pair of cutoffs and a T-shirt with the arms cut out. He looked very strong. "I never turn down a free meal. What time, Dixie?"

"Oh, after the performance. It'll be good. You'll see."

Later that morning Dixie went to watch Val train the tigers. She knew that he never carried a whip to strike them with, just his little baton. When training them, he wore a black pouch on his belt, and every time one of the tigers did a trick right, he would call its name, reach into the pouch, and give it something.

"What's he feeding them? Candy?" she asked.

"No," Helen Langley said. She was wearing a blue summer dress and looked very pretty. "It's little pieces of meat. Every time they do something right, he gives them a piece of meat, and once they get on their stools he never says anything cross or fusses at them."

"Why is that?"

"He wants them to associate sitting on their stools with good things, not bad."

They watched as Val went over and over the tricks.

When finally the session was over, he came out, wiping his face with a towel. "Hello, Helen. Don't you have anything better to do than watch a boring training session?"

Helen smiled—she had a nice smile, Dixie thought—and there was something special in her eyes as she said, "I never get tired of watching you work with the cats. They're so beautiful."

"Well, they're about to drive me crazy."

"What's wrong today?" she asked.

"It's that Stripes. It's so puzzling! His mother was the most teachable tiger I ever had, and he's got the same bloodline. But he's so irritable and snappy. Just like a person who had a lot on his mind and can't sleep. Besides that, he's always got some kind of stomach problem."

"Have you had Doc look at him again?"

"She's as puzzled as I am. She keeps asking about his diet, but he eats the same thing as the rest of the cats."

Dixie stood listening. Then she drifted over to Stripes's cage. He was leaning against the bars, his pale coat gleaming. She reached out and scratched his hindquarters, whispering, "I wish you wouldn't be so bad, Stripes. Why do you do it?"

The huge tiger turned around as though he understood what she was saying. He grunted low in his throat, and Dixie wanted to pet his head, but Val had warned stringently *never* to put her hand inside the cage. "I'm not putting my hand *inside*," she whispered, as she rubbed his coat.

"What are you doing with that old Stripes?"

Dixie turned around to see that Lindsey had come up. "Just petting him," she said. "Isn't he beautiful?"

"No, he's not beautiful!"

"I feel sorry for him. He's sick, and I never could stand to see an animal sick."

Lindsey glared at the tiger. "Well, I hate him!" she said and walked away.

Val and Helen had overheard. Val said, "I don't understand it. She hates that tiger."

"Well, after all, it was Stripes's mother that was responsible for her mother's death."

"Something went wrong that day, and all the cats seemed to go crazy. She just got one scratch, but it turned into blood poisoning."

"You miss her."

"I do. She never liked tigers all that much either."

"But she was in the act with you."

"Just because it was what I did. She was always after me to do something else. Lindsey's the same way now."

Helen glanced after Lindsey. "She blames all tigers for what happened to her mother."

"Don't forget you're coming to supper tonight," Dixie interrupted. She walked away, and her busy little mind was thinking. She had seen the way that Helen Langley had looked at Val. As soon as she got home and started cleaning the trailer, she had it all figured out.

Aunt Sarah came in, wringing wet with sweat. She had been working with the horses, which was hard work.

"Aunt Sarah, did you know that Helen Langley's in love with Val Delaney?"

"Oh, honestly, Dixie—"

"Well, she is! I can just see it when she looks at him."

"You've been seeing too many syrupy movies. Now, I don't want to hear anything more about it!"

Supper was a great success. The trailer was packed. Mooey and Mrs. Sullivan and Mickey were there. Val Delaney came with Lindsey. Even Kirk had come. And Helen.

"I'm surprised that Kirk came," Dixie whispered to Mickey.

"Yeah, he doesn't talk to people much."

"He doesn't bathe much either, but he looks nice tonight."

During the meal, which was mostly Chinese food—Sarah had worked hard on it—everyone seemed to be enjoying the evening. But then Mooey Sullivan leaned over and said, "Now, if you had Mia here, you'd be perfectly happy, wouldn't you, Kirk?"

Kirk flushed. He muttered something, but he was obviously embarrassed. He left soon after the meal.

Mrs. Sullivan said to her husband, "You clumsy Irishman! You ought not to tease that poor young man like that!"

"Well, he's so in love with Mia that he can't see straight!" Mooey protested.

"That makes it all the worse!"

Val was listening, but he said nothing.

Later on, Dixie asked him, "Mr. Delaney, is Kirk really in love with Mia?"

"I think so."

"Is she in love with him?"

"No, she isn't," Lindsey piped up. She was sitting next to her father. "Kirk looked all right tonight when he was all cleaned up, but usually he's dirty, and he smells, and he drinks. Mia's not going to have anything to do with him unless he straightens up."

Val said, "And that's quite enough, Lindsey."

After the meal, Aunt Sarah refused to let anyone work on the dishes. "There's a special on television that we might like."

"Not me. I'm going to play with my dolls," Dixie said. She did not like television specials. She saw Lindsey go over and sit down in front of the television. Then she went back to her bed and began pulling out her Barbies.

"Can I stay back here with you, Dixie?"

Dixie was surprised to see Mickey. He was standing there looking rather helpless. "I don't like television much," he said.

"But you wouldn't want to play with dolls."

"They're right pretty," Mickey said, moving closer.

Dixie was holding Celeste. "They look just like real people, don't they?"

"They're prettier than real people."

"This is Barbie, and this is Ken, and this is Darlene, and this is . . ." She reeled off the names of all the dolls.

Mickey seemed amazed. "You've got all of them named? But they look alike."

"I guess all elephants look alike, but you'd never mistake Ruth for Jean, would you?"

"No . . ."

"Well, I'd never mistake one of my Barbie dolls. They all look different to *me*."

"What do you do with them?"

"I change their clothes. Here, let me show you."

Dixie pulled out box after box of doll clothes. Apparently Mickey had never even seen a Barbie doll up close and was amazed that there were so many different costumes.

"Is that all you do? Just change their clothes?"

"Oh, no! I have them do things together. They've all got relationships."

"What does *that* mean?"

"You see this one? This is Darlene. She's in love with Robert. This is Robert." She held up a boy doll with dark hair. "And this is Robert's sister, Sylvia. She wants to go to medical school, but she can't go because her family doesn't have any money . . ."

Mickey sat down on the bed and picked up a doll. He listened as Dixie explained their problems. "Look," he said finally, "let me move these two around while you make up the stories."

Dixie's eyes sparkled. "Would you, really?"

"Sure. Why not?"

"Most boys don't like dolls."

"I don't care what most boys like. I like to play baseball too. This is just another kind of fun."

"Aren't you afraid you'll be called a sissy?"

"Are *you* going to call me a sissy?"

"No, but Eric would if he found out."

"Who cares what Eric says? Come on, show me how to do it."

Sometimes Aunt Sarah had played dolls with Dixie but not often, because she was busy. Dixie always had to move all the dolls around herself and change their costumes. With Mickey there, it was much more fun.

As for Mickey, he seemed interested in anything new. He'd been fascinated that Dixie knew the names of all the dolls, but soon he knew most of them himself.

They were both surprised when a voice said, "Well, look at this!"

Glancing up, Dixie saw Aunt Sarah smiling down at them.

"Mickey and I have been playing. He knows the names of almost every one of my dolls already."

Mickey scrambled to his feet and grinned. "It was fun. We'll do it again sometime, and maybe you can play ball with me."

"I'd like that," Dixie said.

After everyone had gone, Aunt Sarah said, "That's rather unusual—a boy who isn't embarrassed to play what's been called a girl's game."

"He doesn't care. He's going to be my best friend."

"You couldn't find a better one. But you'd better not tell Eric about the dolls. He'd make Mickey's life miserable."

"He'd better not. I'll—I'll—"

"What will you do?"

"I'll make Ruth pick him up in her trunk and hold him up until he promises to be good!" Dixie exclaimed.

Sarah hugged her. "Don't do anything quite that drastic. But I'm glad you've found a good friend. Everybody needs a good friend."

Dixie suddenly said, "You know what, Aunt Sarah?"

"What?"

"Maybe *you* could fall in love with Val. He's so good-looking, and you could—"

"Now, Dixie, stop that this very minute! I admire Val very much, but that's as far as it's ever going! Now, get these dolls put away, take your shower, and go to bed."

5
MOVING THE BIG TOP

Dixie caught her breath. The climb up the bluff had taken all her strength. At times, the grade had been so steep that she practically had to crawl. But now she was standing on a rock, breathing hard, and looking out over the city of Chattanooga.

Mickey scrambled up beside her. "Boy, this is a grabber, isn't it?"

Dixie was pleased to see that he too was breathing hard.

"This is where the Battle of Lookout Mountain was fought," Helen Langley said. "Come on, Eric," she called.

"All right! Just wait a minute!" Eric yelled, irritable no doubt because he'd been beaten to the top. He clambered up the last few feet. Then, with a sly look, he gave Dixie a sharp bump with his hip.

"Hey!" Dixie almost fell, but Mickey caught her by the arm. Turning to Eric, she said furiously, "Watch what you're doing!"

"Well, if you had the balance that I've got, you wouldn't be falling all over yourself like that." Eric grinned. Then he called, "Hurry up, Lindsey! You going to take all day?"

"Don't pester her, Eric!" Helen said sharply. "She's not in as good condition as you three."

Dixie looked downward as Helen pointed and said, "The Confederates were right along this line here. The Union soldiers were down there in the valley. They had to come up the hill and face the fire of the Southern soldiers."

"Who won?" Eric demanded.

"In this battle the Union soldiers won. Nobody knows exactly what happened, but for one of the few times in the whole war, the Confederates ran away."

"I wouldn't have run away if I had been here!" Eric picked up a stone and threw it. The rock struck near Lindsey. "I'd hit 'em with rocks if nothin' else."

"Be careful! You're liable to hurt Lindsey!" Dixie said sharply.

Lindsey finally arrived at the top, accompanied by Tater, who yapped happily and circled Helen, trying to get her to go farther.

"Be quiet, Tater! This is as far as we're going!"

"Aw, come on," Eric said. "We've got plenty of time before the last show."

"No, we haven't," Helen said. "Anyway, I wanted you to at least see the battlefield."

Mickey was looking at the ground. "It's a little scary to think that right here a man might have died. Right on this spot."

Dixie stared at him in wonder. "You're always thinking things like that. I think it comes from all those books you read."

"No, it comes from playing with dolls," Eric jeered. He had somehow learned about that and had been doing his best to make life miserable for Mickey ever since. "I never heard of a boy playing dolls!"

"People never heard of a girl flying a jet for a long time either," Dixie said, "but now they do!"

"That ain't the same thing as a guy playing with dolls. You're just a sissy, Mickey Sullivan!"

"I am not!" There was anger in Mickey's eyes. "There's nothing wrong with a guy playing with dolls—or cooking either —if he *wants* to!"

The two began to square off.

"All right. No fighting," Helen said quickly. "Let's go down and pick up some brochures about the battle. Then we've got to get back in time for the last show."

After they found some interesting literature on the Battle of Lookout Mountain at the visitors' center, they got into Helen's jeep.

"How come you drive a *jeep?*" Eric asked.

"I just like jeeps," Helen said. "They've got four-wheel drive and can go places that regular cars can't get to. Get away, Tater! Stop licking my ear!"

Dixie, sitting in the backseat and holding Tater, pulled the hound backwards. She stroked his silky ears. "What are Walker hounds good for besides being pets, Miss Helen?"

"They're good hunting dogs. Have a keen sense of smell. My father raised Walker hounds, and I hunted with them when I was a girl."

Finally they pulled into the lot where

the circus trailers were parked, and Mickey said, "Looks like we're just in time."

Dixie ran to get on her costume and be a part of the "Spec," as circus people called the opening parade. It made her feel good to be a part of the circus. She had learned to ride Ruth expertly and had even asked Mooey Sullivan if she could sometimes be in the act. He had smiled, saying, "Why, sure. We'll give you and Ruth a few easy tricks to do."

It was after the final parade, as Dixie started back to change out of her costume, that she met Bigg.

"You better put on your oldest, dirtiest clothes, Dixie. We got to move the Big Top tonight, and that's nothin' but a lot of work!"

Dixie knew that everything had to be packed up. She soon found herself running from one group to another—to the Sullivans, to the Marinos, even to the Von Bulows, helping them get equipment, food for the animals, costumes, and everything else in its proper place.

It was well after midnight when she said to Mickey, "I'm so tired I don't think I can stand up."

"I don't guess you have to, unless you want to watch the Big Top come down."

"I do want to see that!"

The elephants were used to lower the tent. The canvas had to be folded and packed away in the trucks and the collapsing poles put together. Dixie watched for a while, then gave up. She started for the trailer.

On the way she saw Mia putting the last of the Marinos' equipment into a truck. Kirk Delaney was passing by, dirty and with his hair messed up. Dixie heard him say, "Mia?"

"Yes?"

"Would you like to go and get something to eat before we pull out?"

Dixie never knew what Mia would have said, for her father suddenly appeared. "No, she don't have time for that. Be on your way, Delaney!"

Dixie saw the look that passed over Kirk's face, but he left without another word.

Mr. Marino said, "Mia, he's no good and never will be!"

As her father turned away, Dixie thought Mia looked sad. Dixie wanted to go to her and say, "Kirk's not bad. He just needs some help."

She returned to the trailer, so tired she could hardly walk, and got ready for bed. She had just dozed off when she heard the door to the trailer close.

"Are you awake, Dixie?"

"Yes, Aunt Sarah."

"You did very well tonight. I'm proud of you."

"You did fine, too. Are the animals all right?"

"Oh yes."

"What about Stripes?"

"He's still not feeling too well, and I still can't figure it out."

"I wish you could make him well, Aunt Sarah. I love Stripes."

Sarah looked tired. "Val said some tigers just aren't suited for work in the ring. Stripes may have to go to a zoo someday."

This made Dixie sad, and she lay awake for a long time. Finally, she prayed, "Oh, God, I know You care about tigers, for You care about sparrows. Please help Stripes to get well and to be a better tiger . . ."

6

A REAL PUSSYCAT

Two days later Dixie watched the Big Top go back up.

They made the trip to Memphis without incident. The drive was a welcome break for Dixie, and Mickey had ridden with them in the big red truck.

When they reached the lot where the tent was to be, Dixie watched Ruth and the other elephants go to work. They were harnessed, and when the big pole was ready to go up, it was the elephants that raised it.

"Oh, isn't it exciting!" Dixie exclaimed as she saw the tent take shape.

"I've seen it so many times, I'm used to it," Mickey said.

She wandered into the Big Top and watched the roustabouts put the trapeze in place. Mr. Marino was there, supervising them.

Dixie walked over to where Mia was standing beside Brett Bailey and listened to them talk a while. When Brett left, Dixie moved closer and said, "Mia? I want to ask you something."

Mia was an attractive girl in perfect physical condition. She had dark hair and dark eyes like her father. She smiled. "What is it, Dixie?"

"Do you like Kirk Delaney?"

The question seemed to take Mia off guard. Her face grew red. "Why do you ask that?"

"It's just that I know he likes you. He watches you all the time when he's not handling the tigers. Every time you go up to do your act, he gets as close as he can."

Mia said nothing.

"Well, I know he *looks* pretty bad sometimes," Dixie went on. "But I think he could be a real good man if . . ."

Mia gave her a sharp look. "Did Kirk ask you to talk to me?"

"Oh, no! He'd never do anything like that. I just feel sorry for him."

Mia bit her lip, and there was silence

for a long time. Then she said, "I feel sorry for him, too, but—"

"He was in love with somebody once, wasn't he?"

Mia's eyes flew open. "Well, you've learned a lot of gossip since you've been with the circus." She ran a hand over her hair and seemed unable to say more for a moment. "Yes," she said finally, "he was. Long ago. After she decided to marry someone else, Kirk was never the same again. It's a shame because—"

When she broke off, Dixie looked up quickly. "Because you like him?"

"It wouldn't do me any good to like him," Mia said sadly. "My father would never let me have anything to do with a failure. Papa is a perfectionist." She looked up to where Mr. Marino was trying out the trapeze overhead. "You *have* to be a perfectionist to be up there. Just one split second off, and somebody can be dead. So he expects everybody to be perfect."

"Nobody's perfect."

"I know that, but Papa doesn't."

"Look, Lindsey, isn't that pretty?"

Lindsey was playing with Tater near

the tiger cage. She looked up to see what Dixie was talking about. "It's nothing but Lena jumping through a hoop."

"I know, but isn't she beautiful!" Dixie exclaimed. She watched the tiger jump again through the hoop Val was holding. "Just think how hard it is to get a tiger to do something like that. It's not natural for tigers to jump through hoops."

Lindsey was trying to keep Tater from licking her face. "I don't see what's so wonderful about it."

By this time Dixie had become accustomed to the fact that Lindsey was not going to show excitement over anything the tigers did. However, she never gave up trying.

"I think Helen's such a nice lady, don't you?" she said, changing the subject.

"She's all right."

"I mean, not many people would have taken us to Lookout Mountain. And she's always real helpful. I think she likes you a lot, Lindsey."

Lindsey scowled. "She wants to marry Daddy. But she's not my mother!"

Dixie did not know exactly how to answer this. She saw that Lindsey was sharp enough to know that Helen did like her father. But one look at the scowl on her face and Dixie knew it was a hopeless conversation.

"Well, I think she's very nice. Like I say, she likes you a lot."

"I don't need anybody to like me, except my father. And if I could get him away from this circus, we could have a regular life instead of traipsing all over the country like we do."

Dixie said, "Well, I don't have a regular life either, Lindsey. My parents are off in Africa. And even when I go to be with them, it won't be a 'regular life.'"

Lindsey looked at her curiously. "Are you really going to Africa?"

"As soon as my parents get everything ready. Dad says it's too hard for children to be in the place where they are now."

"What's it like in Africa? Never mind. Don't tell me! I'd hate it. I want to live in a nice American town in a nice house, and I want my dad to be home every night."

Eyeing Lindsey, Dixie could not think of anything else to say on this subject. So she suggested, "Why don't you come over to the trailer, and we'll play with my dolls?"

"I'll have to do that later. I've got a tutoring session. I've got to do math lessons, even in summer. Bigg is tutoring me."

"Does he know math?"

"He's a shark," Lindsey said, her eyes lighting up. "You wouldn't think a little fellow like that would know so much."

"I guess size doesn't have anything to do with how much people know. Big people can be pretty dumb."

Lindsey got up and pushed Tater away. "Go on, Tater. Leave me alone now." She walked off, and Tater immediately transferred his affections to Dixie.

She played with the dog for a while, and then Val came out of the tiger cage, wiping the sweat from his face.

"Mr. Delaney, I wish I could help with the tigers. I just love them!"

"Do you, Dixie?"

"They're so beautiful!" She let her eyes run over the big cats. Two of them were playing like kittens. She looked up suddenly and said, "Do you suppose there *is* any way I could help?"

"Well, I've been thinking about getting Lindsey into the act. That would be a sight to see—a young girl in the cage with a four-hundred-pound tiger, but"—his face suddenly grew sad—"she's just not interested in tigers."

"Could *I* do it, do you think?"

Val studied her face. "I don't believe your aunt would ever let you do it."

"I'll bet she would if it were safe enough somehow."

"I couldn't ever let you in the cage with some of the cats—like Stripes, for instance. He's too moody. But on the other hand—" A thought seemed to come to him, and he reached into the cage and rubbed a tiger on the head. "Salome here, she's a real pussycat."

"She's expecting cubs, Aunt Sarah says."

"Yes, she is, and maybe that's when you can help."

"How?" Dixie asked eagerly.

"Well, tiger cubs take lots of care." He began to talk about how the circus had to get its tigers. "Years ago, tigers could be imported from India and a few other places, but not anymore. They're an endangered species. They're being killed off very quickly."

"That's sad!" Dixie exclaimed.

"It *is* sad. So now we have to breed our own, and I hope old Salome has a big litter. But the cubs are a lot of work."

Dixie came closer. "Could I pet her on the head?"

"You wouldn't be afraid?"

"Not if you tell me what to do."

"All right. Come on." He guided Dixie's hand, keeping his own inside the cage on the tiger's head.

"This is Dixie, Salome. She's going to be your friend."

Dixie ran her hand down the side of the tigress, feeling the massive muscles and the rough coat. Then she moved her hand upward, and while Val tickled Salome under the jaw, she stroked the massive head.

"I want to help," she said. "I can't ever be a lion tamer, but I know I could take care of the cubs."

"That's a bargain," Val said quickly.

"What about Stripes?"

Val frowned. "I guess your aunt's told you—we still just don't know what's the matter with him. He's always got stomach trouble, and he's irritable. And he's one of the most nervous cats I've ever seen. It's a shame. His mother was a fine tigress."

"I prayed for Stripes last night."

"Did you, now? You think God will answer you?"

Dixie looked up into the animal trainer's handsome face. "He says He'll give us the desires of our heart, and my desire is to see Stripes become a good, obedient tiger."

"Amen," Val Delaney said. He put his hand on Dixie's head. "I'll just join you in that prayer, Dixie."

7

THREE FINE BABIES

Ooooh, those are *nasty!*"

Lindsey Delaney held onto the side of the bobbing boat and stared at the small pieces of whitish meat that Kirk held out to her. "I don't even want to touch that stuff!"

Lindsey's Uncle Kirk grinned broadly and reached into a bucket, bringing up more pieces of bait. "It's nothing but squid. Why, over in Japan they think this is good eating."

"I don't care!" Lindsey shuddered.

Suddenly the white boat took a plunge, and the captain yelled, "OK, hurry and let down! We're right in the middle of the biggest school of fish I ever saw!"

Dixie held her fishing rod awkwardly and released the brake. The heavy weight began to pull the line out, and she held on with both hands. It seemed to go down for a long, long way. And then the line went slack.

Quickly, as Kirk had showed her, she threw the brake on, reeled in three turns, and then waited. "I hope I get a big one!" she cried to Mickey, standing beside her.

After they had been in Mobile, Alabama, for two days, Kirk brought up the idea of a fishing expedition. And now here they were, out in the Gulf of Mexico, bobbing about in the brilliant green sparkling water. Small whitecaps were all around. Overhead the skies were a hard blue, and fluffy white clouds drifted along the skyline.

The fishing party included Dixie, Mickey, Lindsey, and Eric. Along with Kirk and Val and Helen Langley, they lined the rail that went around the sides and back of the small rented boat. The smell of salt air was keen in Dixie's nose, and she was delighted that she had not gotten seasick, as Eric had told her she would.

And then she felt a hard tug on her line. "I got one!" she yelled and—again as Kirk had taught her—brought up the end of the pole with a mighty jerk. It seemed to be hung up on something, and she said, "I'm stuck!"

"No, you're not." Kirk came over. He

was wearing a pair of white cutoffs and was tanned a deep mahogany. He looked very strong and rather handsome without the dirty clothes he usually wore. "Crank it up. Let's see what you got!" He showed her how to simply raise the pole and then turn the reel very quickly as she lowered it.

After a long struggle, Mickey said, "I see it! It's a big one!"

Dixie's arms were tired, but she was so excited she hardly noticed. She too had seen the outline of the fish underwater, and it looked enormous. "What is it, Kirk?" she yelled.

"A big snapper." He picked up a net, and when Dixie hauled her catch close to the surface, he slipped it under the struggling fish. Then he deposited net and fish on deck, where the snapper flopped wildly.

"Oh, it's so big!" Dixie cried. She put down the pole and came to where Kirk was taking the fish out of the net. It was a brilliant red.

He said, "It'll probably go ten pounds. That's big enough to have mounted, unless you want to eat it."

"I want to have it mounted!"

"Aw, who wants an old dead fish on the

wall?" Eric said, probably mad that he had not caught the fish himself. But right away he got a bite and began reeling it in.

For the next thirty minutes, everyone caught fish. Dixie caught two more, not as large as the first one. Mickey caught an ugly-looking thing that looked like a snake with a round mouth.

"Don't let that thing on board!" Val yelled. "It's a sucker eel!"

Deftly he removed the ugly creature from the hook and tossed it over the side. "They fasten themselves onto the bottom of fish and feed until they kill the fish," he said. Then he turned to Lindsey, who was just watching. "Come on, honey," he said, "I'll hold the pole for you."

"I don't want to, Daddy."

Dixie saw the disappointment that flashed in Val Delaney's eyes, and she thought, *He's tried everything to give Lindsey a good time. I wish she would show a little bit more gratitude.*

A little later Helen said, "We'd better be getting back, if we're going to make the night show. Besides, some of us are going to get burned. Look." She held out an arm, which was already turning pink.

"I guess we've got enough," Kirk said. "Head for the barn, Captain."

The captain, a sawed-off, round individual who smoked a huge cigar constantly, seemed surprised. "We can get more," he replied.

"No, this is enough. Let's go back."

When the captain nudged the boat into its slot at the marina, he said, "I can get somebody to clean those fish for you."

"That's all right, Captain," Kirk said. "I always liked to clean fish."

The captain took the cigar out of his mouth. "I never heard of anyone who *liked* to clean fish. Some of us like to eat 'em, and others like to catch 'em, but not clean 'em."

Kirk's teeth were white against his tan as he laughed. "I guess I'm just born to do the unusual."

He gathered up all the fish in the two large white buckets that the captain provided. They took Dixie's fish to have it mounted, and then the party started back to the circus grounds.

As soon as they got there, Dixie said, "Can I help you clean the fish?"

"It's a pretty nasty job, Dixie," Kirk said.

"I don't mind."

Dixie and Mickey followed Kirk behind the tent to the area where there was a faucet. Eric and Lindsey disappeared, and Kirk grinned. "I didn't think they'd want any of this kind of work."

They watched him pick up a big fish and a long, sharp-looking knife. "This is a fillet knife," he said. In just minutes, he was holding up a large chunk of red fish. "And this is what we call a fillet," he announced. "No bones in it. Just good meat."

Flipping the fish over, he cut the fillet from the other side and tossed the fish head and skin and skeleton into a bucket. "Anybody want to try it?" He grinned.

"I don't think so," Dixie decided. "Do you, Mickey?"

"Sure, I'll try."

But Mickey made such a mess that Kirk just laughed and took the fillet knife away. "Why don't you two just watch?"

They had gotten back early enough for Helen to fry the fish. When Dixie and Mickey returned to her trailer, they found her waiting with a cooker already hot.

"This is going to be the freshest fish I ever had," she said. She took some of the fillets, rolled them in cornmeal, and dropped them into the bubbling grease. "Watch out, now. Don't let it pop over on you."

Helen was an expert, Dixie discovered, at cooking fish. She had made hush puppies, round balls of cornmeal dough, that she popped into the boiling fat and let Dixie fish out with a wire strainer.

Finally it was all ready, and they sat down at an outside table to eat. Just as they did, Mia Marino walked by.

Helen cast a quick glance at Kirk, then called, "Come join us, Mia. We've got plenty of fish."

Mia looked over at the group. "I don't want to intrude," she said, her eyes on Kirk.

"Come on," Val encouraged her. "Here, you can sit down between two good-looking men." He winked at Kirk, who was sitting next to him. "Move over, Kirk. Let Mia in there."

Kirk flushed and got up. "I'm not really hungry. You can have my place, Mia." He walked off.

Dixie's eyes met Helen's. It was as if they shared a secret, but neither of them said anything right then.

Mia watched Kirk disappear. Then she said shortly, "No, thanks. I'm not really very hungry either."

As she walked away, Eric picked up a piece of fish and bit into it. Apparently it was so hot it burned his mouth. He spat it out and began yelling, his face red.

"If you weren't so piggish," Mickey said, "you wouldn't get burned! Here's the way to eat fish." He cut off a bit with a knife, impaled it with a fork, blew on it, and then put it in his mouth. "Boy, that is good fish!"

"Dip it in some of this tartar sauce," Dixie said. "That's the way we always ate it at home."

They could not eat all the fish, so Tater came in for his share. Helen broke off small bits and made him perform his tricks. Tater could sit up, speak, and roll over. Then she said, "I taught him a new trick. Sit, Tater."

The Walker hound sat on his haunches and held his nose up. "Still, Tater," Helen said. She broke off a piece of fish and balanced it on his nose. "Don't move," she cautioned.

Dixie watched with delight as Tater sat with the fish on his nose. She could almost see his mouth water.

Then Helen snapped her fingers. Instantly the dog moved, and the fish was gone down his throat. He wagged his whole body violently and nudged Helen for more.

Val grinned. "We might put him in the act. You think he'd like to be in a cageful of tigers, Helen?"

"You're not putting *my* dog in with those cats!" Helen said.

As the two began talking about the act, Dixie again thought it was a shame that her scheme to get them married off had come to nothing. *But I'm not through,* she said to herself. *They just need a little encouragement.*

Then everyone pitched in to clean up after the feast.

Later that night, Dixie made a rather unusual discovery. She was passing the Sullivans' trailer when Mrs. Sullivan called out, "Dixie, come here!"

"What is it, Miss Irene?"

"I cooked up chicken livers, and I made way too many. Take these, and you and the doc can have them, if you like them."

Actually, Dixie did not like chicken livers, and she knew that Aunt Sarah didn't either, but it would have been impolite to say so. "Thank you very much, Miss Irene," she said, taking the container.

She headed for the trailer, taking a

shortcut through the menagerie tent. As she passed by Stripes's cage, she saw him lying down and staring at her with his big green eyes. A thought came to her. Stepping close to the cage, she said, "Do *you* like chicken livers, Stripes?"

The big tiger opened his mouth and seemed to nod. She knew he had not understood her, but she took out one of the chicken livers and held it up.

The nose of the big Siberian tiger twitched. He growled deep in his chest, but it was not an angry sound.

"Here you go!" Dixie tossed it in.

Stripes immediately picked up the liver with his tongue and opened his mouth for more.

"Oh, you *like* chicken livers! Well, here. You can have another one." Dixie fed more livers to the tiger and then wondered if they were good for him.

"Well, if they're good for people," she said to the tiger, "I guess they're good for tigers. Here, take another one." Soon, despite what she had been told, she got so close that the tiger's big tongue brushed against her hand. It startled her, but Stripes liked the livers so much that she could not imagine his hurting her. Soon she'd fed him all of them, and still he begged for more.

"That's all I have now, but I'll tell you what, Stripes. I'll buy you some livers with my own money. See if I don't!"

Dixie heard a voice, and someone was knocking on the side of the trailer. Her eyes seemed to be stuck together, and she struggled to come out of a deep sleep.

"Doc! Wake up, Doc!"

Forcing her eyes open, Dixie sat up in bed. She looked toward the front of the trailer. Aunt Sarah had stumbled out of her own bed and was going to the door. Dixie heard her say, "Who is it?"

"It's me, Val Delaney. You've got to come, Doc! It's Salome—she's about to have her cubs."

"I'll be right there!"

"Better hurry! I don't think there's much time!"

Dixie scrambled out of bed, too, and began pulling on her clothes.

"What are you doing, Dixie?" Aunt Sarah demanded, as she dressed.

"I'm going with you, Aunt Sarah."

"Well . . . all right, but you'll have to be quiet and stay out of the way."

"I promise."

Dixie dressed quickly, pulling on a pair of jeans and a knitted green T-shirt. She slipped her feet into her Keds and was ready and waiting when Sarah grabbed her bag and started out the door.

"Let's go," she said. "I've never delivered tiger cubs before."

She sounded somewhat nervous, so Dixie said, "You'll do fine, Aunt Sarah."

They hurried through the darkness, threading their steps between the trailers. When they came to the tiger cages in the menagerie tent, the animals seemed to be restless.

Val met them. "I've handled this myself a time or two, but I never feel good about it, Doc. I'm glad you're here."

Sarah said, "And I've never had any experience, but I guess it's time I learn."

Val led them to a separate part of the tent, away from the rest of the animals. Dixie swallowed hard when her aunt went with Val into Salome's cage.

After a while, Sarah came out to get something. She said, "You might as well go back to bed, Dixie. This may take all night after all."

"No, I don't want to do that."

"Then go back and make some coffee. Put it in the Thermos, and bring it to us. Bring some sugar and cream too."

Glad to have something to do, Dixie ran back to the trailer. It did not take long to heat water and make the coffee. She poured it into the stainless steel jug, screwed the lid on tight, and picked up some packets of sugar and cream.

She started back. It was a dark night— there was no moon—so she stumbled over several tent pegs. She bit her lip to keep from crying out and kept on going.

As she passed by the line of cages that the tigers occupied, she halted abruptly, for one of the tigers was growling in an unusual way. She strained her eyes in the darkness, and then she saw someone standing by one of the cages. Dixie could not see what he was doing, but when she stepped a little closer, she saw that whoever it was had a stick and was poking at the tiger.

"What are you doing?" Dixie yelled before she could think.

Instantly the shadowy figure ducked out of sight and disappeared.

Running up, Dixie saw that it had been Stripes who was being tormented. She watched him pace back and forth, then saw that someone had thrown some sort of food into his cage. Dixie ran on. She would tell Val about it.

When she delivered the coffee, however, Val was busy, so she said nothing. Instead, she sat down and waited nervously.

An hour later, Val and her aunt came out of the cage. Each was holding something.

Dixie stood up. "Are they born?" she asked excitedly.

"They sure are. You want to hold one?" Val asked.

He handed her a small ball of fur, and Dixie crooned with delight. "It's so little!"

"When he gets big, he'll weigh five or six hundred pounds." Val grinned. "Enjoy him while you can."

"This one is a boy?"

"That's one of the boys. Why don't you name him?"

"Can I really do that?"

"Sure. A royal name."

Dixie thought hard. "I name you Prince."

"A good name," Val said. He turned to Sarah and grinned again. "Now, it's your treat, Doc. You name that one."

"All right, little lady. What will I name you?" Aunt Sarah held up the small tiger and said, "I think I'll name you Queenie."

"Great name." Val held out the remaining tiger, hesitated, then said, "And I name you Rajah—Prince, Rajah, and Queenie."

"They're going to take lots of care, aren't they, Mr. Delaney?"

"You wouldn't believe how much. Most of the time baby tigers have to be raised on a bottle. Nobody knows why, but tiger cubs are rejected by their mothers about 80 percent of the time."

"I'll help. I promised I would, and you said I could."

"I'm not turning down any help I can get." He held up his tiger cub again, and a smile crossed his face. "We're going to have lots of fun, you and me."

Dixie held her tiny cub close, cuddling it as if it were a baby. "And we're going to have lots of fun, too," she whispered.

8

THE CIRCUS AT WORK

All the next day, Dixie thought of little else but the three cubs. But late that night she began to see what Val had meant when he said, "Cubs are harder to take care of than babies."

"I promised Val I'd give the cubs their midnight feeding, Aunt Sarah," she said at bedtime. "Will I wake you up if I set my clock?"

"It doesn't matter. If you've given your word, you'll need to do it. Be sure you take the flashlight."

"I will."

Dixie went to sleep quickly, and when the alarm sounded she found it difficult to awaken. She was tempted to shut off the alarm and go back to sleep, but she forced herself to get up. She sat on the edge of the bed, trying to open her eyes, then switched on the small bed light. She pulled on jeans and a blue shirt. She buttoned the shirt up wrong and had to start over. Her hair was awry. She gave it a few brushes. Then, picking up the flashlight and a container of chicken livers—in case Stripes was awake —she left the trailer.

Overhead the stars were bright, and she began to awaken as she walked past the silent trailers. At the menagerie tent, she went to where the cubs were kept in their special cage. They were mewing and crying. She said, "I'll be with you in just a minute."

Val had showed her how to fix formula, and she heated it on the small electric burner. When it was warm, she tested it on her wrist, then filled the bottles and entered the cage. Sitting down with the cubs, she cooed as they stumbled blindly against her. They were like house kittens and gave little hint of the tremendous size that would be theirs when they were grown.

She picked up Queenie, saying, "Ladies first," and popped the nipple into the cub's mouth. Queenie pawed at the bottle and sucked greedily. The milk ran down her chin as she drank, and the other two baby tigers crawled, whining, into Dixie's lap.

"All right, Prince, it's your turn." She fed him and then Rajah. When the last cub had drunk all the formula, she felt his stomach. It was round and swollen. "That's a good boy!"

Dixie petted the cubs awhile. They went to sleep almost at once, and it was quiet in the tent. She sat thinking about how strange her life had become since her parents had gone to the mission field.

It was warm in the tent, and she began to be sleepy. Putting her head back, she dozed off and began to dream. She dreamed of Barbie dolls. Then she dreamed of her parents in faraway Africa. She was awakened when a voice called her name.

"Dixie?"

Opening her eyes and straightening with a jolt, Dixie looked up to see Val squatting on his heels and smiling at her.

"Oh, Mr. Delaney!" Dixie said. She looked at the three kittens cuddled in her lap. Her legs were asleep. "I can't even feel my feet."

Laughing, Val picked up Rajah. "Looks

like these fellas are full."

"They ate all their formula."

"That's good, Dixie."

"Mr. Delaney, why won't Salome keep her cubs? All the cats I know were good to their kittens."

"As I told you, most of the time female tigers in captivity won't nurse their young. Nobody knows why. I don't think it's that way out in the wild. When my first tigress had her cubs, I left them with her—and she killed them right after birth."

"How awful!"

"It really shook me," Val admitted. "Since then, I separate the cubs from their mother just as soon as they are born."

"It's a good thing I'm here. I can be their mother."

He grinned. "That's good, because there's one part of tiger motherhood that's a little hard to imitate."

"What's that, Mr. Delaney?"

"Well, I'm sure you know that one of the more unpleasant jobs of taking care of human babies is changing diapers."

"Oh, I don't mind that. I changed my niece's diapers."

"Here's the way tigers work, Dixie.

Something about the way that a mother tiger licks her cubs causes them to have bowel movements. If they don't get that licking, they don't have them."

"You mean they get constipated?"

"That's right, and it can be very serious."

Dixie stared at the cubs. "You don't mean I'm going to have to lick them, do you?"

Val grinned. "No," he said. "There's a way to get around it. What you do is this." He held Rajah in one hand and began rubbing the cub's backside in a downward motion. Rajah immediately awoke and sent up an abrasive, squawking noise that disturbed the other kittens.

"Does it hurt him?" Dixie asked.

"I don't think it does," Val said. "But in any case, he has to have it. All three of them do. Why don't you try Queenie there?"

Queenie did not like the massage any more than her brother. Nevertheless, Dixie firmly held her, saying, "Now, you be quiet, Queenie. This is good for you."

After Val was sure that Dixie had learned the method of massaging the cubs, he said, "You're doing fine. I wish Lindsey

103

would take an interest in the cubs the way you do."

"I think she gets lonesome," Dixie said. She took a deep breath and then said, "I think she misses her mother."

"I know she does." Val fondled Rajah's head, then looked off into the dark recesses of the tent. "I do, too," he said quietly. "I get pretty lonesome."

Dixie had an impulse to do a little matchmaking right then but remembered what Aunt Sarah had said about minding her own business, so she said nothing.

"You may as well go back and get some sleep, Dixie. The next feeding will be at six o'clock."

"And I'll do it," Dixie said eagerly. "I don't mind getting up early."

"Are you sure? It gets to be quite a grind."

"Just let me do it, Mr. Delaney."

She headed back to the trailer, and it was still dark. As she passed through the menagerie tent, she stopped to see Stripes. Peering in, she saw him lying in the back of his cage. She held out a chicken liver and said, "Come on, Stripes, here's your livers."

Ordinarily he came at once, but this time he did not even raise his head. Then she noticed something between his paws. He was eating. This puzzled Dixie, for it was not feeding time, and she wondered if it had been left over.

But that hardly ever happens, she thought. *They eat everything that's given to them. I wish I could get in there and see what he's eating.*

As she turned away, she saw a figure and recognized Kirk.

"Hello, Kirk," she said.

"Hello, Dixie, what are you doing up at this time of night?"

"I came over to feed the cubs. It's awful early for you, isn't it?"

"Couldn't sleep."

"Kirk, look. I brought Stripes some chicken livers."

"Chicken livers?"

"I found out he loves them. But when I tried to give him some just now, he wouldn't eat. Look, he's got something in there between his paws. It's happened before."

Kirk went to the cage and peered into the shadows. "I guess he has. Maybe some food left over . . ." He turned back to Dixie and said, "You sure like that tiger, don't you?"

"I'm worried about him, Kirk. He seems sick all the time, and he's irritated."

"He'll be all right." Kirk seemed moody. He walked away.

Dixie watched him go, and the thought popped into her mind, *He acts funny. Like he knew something about whatever it is that Stripes is eating. I wonder if he's feeding Stripes something to make him sick. But why?*

Dixie thought she would tell Aunt Sarah at breakfast but decided not to. The two ate pancakes in the trailer, and after her aunt left to begin her duties, Dixie turned on the TV. There were cartoons on, and she watched the small figures doing absurd things, but all the time she was thinking about the Delaneys and how messed up their lives were.

"It's just like one of those soap operas," she said. "I hate those things, but sometimes real people get messed up, too."

The sound of the circus band filled the tent. As always, when Dixie heard the music, her pulse began to beat faster. She had learned to love almost everything about the circus.

For nearly a week she'd missed a great deal of sleep, for she had faithfully done the night feedings for the three cubs. They recognized her and scrambled over her eagerly as she fed them. They had *not* learned to like the massaging of their backsides, but Val told her, "You're doing a fine job. One way we can tell tiger cubs are healthy is by examining their bowel movements."

That way, Dixie learned, he knew whether they needed more cereal in their diet. She learned to mix it with their milk, and by this time the cubs were able to eat not only from the bottle but also clumsily from a bowl.

She walked into the Big Top as the Chinese family, the Los, were performing. Sidney Lo was a juggler, and right now he had what seemed to be fifty balls in the air. Dixie watched entranced, for she had tried to juggle and could not even do three.

Soon Wani, Sidney's daughter, who was no older than Dixie, came on. She was not only a juggler but also a contortionist. Dixie watched, holding her breath, as Wani seemed to tie herself in knots. "It's like she doesn't have any bones!" Dixie whispered to herself. When the Los came off after taking their bows, Dixie hugged the girl. "You did fine, Wani."

"Thank you, Dixie." Wani was slender with large, lustrous eyes. "How are the cubs?"

"Oh, doing fine. After the act, come over and I'll show them to you. You can help me feed them."

"All right." Wani waited with Dixie at the edge of the cage that had been set up for the next act.

Charles Rielly, the ringmaster, filled the tent with his big booming voice. "And now for the most death-defying act on the planet! I give you the Great Delaney and his Siberian tigers!"

Dixie and Wani watched as most of the lights went out under the Big Top. All the spots were focused on the big, white, pale-striped tigers as they came out of their slot and went immediately to their low, wooden perches. Val was waving his baton, speaking to each one.

"See how he gives each one a little bite of meat when they get on their perches," Wani said.

"Yes, he doesn't believe in punishing them," Dixie said. "He doesn't want them to grow to hate their stools."

As the act went on, Dixie kept her eye especially on Stripes. She was worried about him, for he'd come slinking out with his head down, not like the others, who bounded into the cage with energy and enthusiasm.

"What's wrong with Stripes?" Wani asked. "He looks sick."

"I think he is," Dixie murmured. She could hear Val bragging on each tiger in a soft voice. He would stop from time to time to rub one's head, and they all performed well. Without protest, three of the tigers even did the leap through the flaming hoop—which they did not really like.

The act was almost over when Leo, the largest tiger, passed close to Stripes. Dixie could not see what happened, but either Leo made a swipe at Stripes or Stripes decided to jump on the other tiger. In any case, suddenly the Big Top was filled with a fierce roar, and the two tigers were nothing but a blur.

"Oh, he's killing him!" Dixie cried out. She wanted to run and help but knew there was nothing she could do. She saw Val, shouting for help, run to where the two tigers were clawing and biting each other fiercely. He grabbed the head of one of them. It proved to be Leo, and Leo, with one mighty blow of his paw, caught Val in the middle of the back. The impact knocked him flat.

The two tigers continued to fight. They might have killed each other, but Kirk suddenly appeared with a water hose, which he turned on the two fighting animals. Sputtering and blinded, they tucked their tails and separated.

Val slowly got to his feet and directed the tigers into their cages. Stripes was the last to go. He growled at Val but lowered his head and slunk away.

Dixie and Wani went backstage at once. When they got there, Helen was already stripping away Val's shirt. There were four long furrows right across his back.

Helen drew a short breath. "I know that hurts, but we'll have to put some antiseptic on it."

"Do I need stitches?"

"No, but we'll have to be sure it doesn't

get infected. You know how dirty their claws get."

Dixie and Wani huddled around while Helen, with trembling fingers, cleaned the wound and applied antiseptic. She then taped on bandages, saying, "I'll have to change this two or three times a day, Val."

"Thanks," Val said. "It looks like I need a keeper myself."

"I don't mind," Helen said. "I can't tell you how frightened I was when you jumped into that fight. They both could have turned on you."

Dixie said, "I was scared, too, Mr. Delaney. It's a good thing Kirk was there."

"It sure is." Val looked over at his brother, who was soothing the tigers. "Hey, Kirk. Thanks a lot, buddy."

"That's all right. You'd do the same for me."

All might have been well, but Lindsey chose this moment to enter. She went straight to her father, and her lips trembled. She said, "I thought you were going to be killed."

"It wasn't that bad, sweetheart."

"It was awful! You know you could have been killed! You know it!"

Val gave the girl a despairing look. He tried to put his arms around her, but she pushed him away. "Daddy, please don't go into those tiger cages again. Let's leave the circus. You can get a job doing something else."

"This is my job, honey. It's what I do."

"You could quit!"

Val tried to answer, but Lindsey was past listening to reason. When she saw that he was not going to agree, she turned away, her face white. "I hate the circus, and I hate those tigers!" She left with her back stiff.

"I'll go see if I can talk to her, Val," Helen said quickly.

As soon as Helen was gone, Dixie whispered to Wani, "She misses her mother."

"She was a nice lady," Wani said. "I can remember her. She always was sweet to all the children in the circus."

"Maybe Val needs to get another wife."

"I don't know," Wani said doubtfully. "It'd be hard for another woman to move into that family."

That night, after the last show, Dixie and her aunt were going back toward their trailer when Helen stopped them.

"Something's wrong with Tater, Sarah. Do you think you can take a look at him?"

"Why, of course. What is it?"

On the way to the trailer, Helen explained Tater's ailments.

The dog was tied at the trailer door. Dixie watched as her aunt took the animal's temperature and examined him.

"I don't think it's serious."

"That's good," Helen said. "I don't need any more trouble. I've got enough of that."

They went back to their own trailer, and Dixie got ready for bed. When she lay down, Sarah came to pray with her as usual. Before she had a chance, however, Dixie said, "I want Val to marry Helen— then the Delaneys could have a real family."

Sarah looked shocked. She glanced at the Barbie doll that lay on Dixie's pillow and then put her hand on Dixie's. "Honey," she said, "you must *stop* meddling in other people's business."

"But Lindsey needs a mother, and Val needs a wife."

"That may be, but they'll have to work that out for themselves." Aunt Sarah hesitated, then said, "Honey, people aren't Barbie dolls. You can do with dolls as you like, and no harm is done. But when you try to interfere with people's lives, you can do a great deal of damage."

"But I love the Delaneys. I want to see them happy."

"So do I, Dixie, but they'll just have to work out their problems for themselves. What we *can* do is pray for them."

Dixie murmured, "All right," and she did pray for the Delaneys. But as she went to sleep that night, she was still trying to find a way to make Val Delaney see how all his problems would be solved if he would just marry Helen Langley.

"What was that about a butcher?"

"Somebody that sells hot dogs and sodas." Bigg laughed. "If you'd put down those cubs for a while, maybe you'd learn more about the rest of the circus."

"This is my job," Dixie said firmly.

"And from what Val tells me, you're doing a good job. Got to go."

Dixie finished feeding and massaging the cubs. They growled and chewed on her fingers.

Then she got up and left them, passing by Stripes's cage. Reaching into the pouch at her waist, she pulled out some chicken livers and tossed them to him.

This time he came over at once and put the top of his head against the bars. It had become a habit of his. He seemed to like her.

She scratched the top of his head and fed him more livers. When they were gone, he growled and looked at her with his beautiful green eyes. Dixie whispered, "I wish I could come in the cage and pet you, but Mr. Delaney says I can't do that. Well, I'll be back with some more chicken livers before long."

The next day was Sunday. Dixie put on

9

DIXIE GOES TO CHURCH

Hey, first of May! Tell the butcher stay away from the bulls! We ha some cherry pie for him before doors!"

Dixie stopped feeding Rajah looked up with astonishment at Bigg, had popped into the menagerie ten don't understand a word of that! Wha you talking about, Bigg?"

Bigg was in his clown outfit. He gr at her. "You have to learn how to talk talk, Dixie. First of May is somebody circus work. That's from when they in the old days, don't you see?"

"Oh. Well, then, what's all tha cherry pie and doors?"

"Well, doors means the crowd' in to take their seats. Cherry pie, means extra work."

her nicest dress, a green cotton print. Aunt Sarah dressed up, too. Then they went to the Big Top, where a group of performers and roustabouts were gathered for a morning church service.

She sat down beside Mickey. He was wearing a pair of jeans with a checkered shirt, and Dixie thought he looked very nice. "I hope your dad's got a good sermon this morning."

"You need one!" a voice said.

Dixie glanced over at Eric, who was grinning in his usual cocky fashion. She had to admit that he was a fine-looking boy with his blond hair and brilliant blue eyes, but he was so mean to her most of the time that that didn't matter.

They had no time to say more, for Mooey Sullivan got up and said, "We're going to sing some hymns now." Glancing over his congregation, he grinned. "Let's hear you songbirds sing out. The first song is 'What a Friend We Have in Jesus.'"

Dixie knew that song and sang as loudly as she could. She joined in on the rest of them too, for they were all old hymns that she had learned while attending church with her parents.

When the singing was over, Mr. Sullivan picked up his Bible. "Now I'm going to talk to you this morning on the prodigal son."

"I've heard that sermon," Eric grumbled.

"Oh, quiet, Eric!" Mickey snapped. "You need to hear it!"

"I don't need it any more than you do!" Eric grunted. "Just because you're the preacher's kid, you don't need to think you're better than the rest of us!"

"Both of you hush!" Mrs. Sullivan leaned over and rapped Mickey on the head with her finger. "You be quiet, Mickey, and you too, Eric."

Dixie listened as the big elephant trainer spoke. As he talked about how the prodigal son wasted all that he had and finally wound up eating garbage with the hogs, she happened to notice Kirk Delaney.

Kirk was standing back in the shadow of the grandstand. He was still wearing his dirty work clothes. His hair was messy, and his eyes were bleary. From time to time his eyes would go to Mia Marino, who was very pretty in a white dress with a spray of red flowers pinned to one shoulder.

Dixie's fertile brain once again went into action. *If he'd just dress up, he'd look so nice. And I don't know why he has to drink. What he needs is Jesus to fix up his life.* She thought, *I wish it was as easy to put people where they belong as it is my dolls. I could fix all of Kirk's problems if I could just do that.*

After the service, Dixie went back to where he stood. "It was a good sermon, wasn't it?"

"It was all right," Kirk muttered. He was watching Mia again, but he pulled his eyes away from her to look at Dixie. "You look real nice, Dixie."

"Thanks, Kirk." She called him by his first name, which she never would have done with Val. Then she said, as if a thought had just occurred to her, "Doesn't Mia look pretty this morning?"

Kirk turned his eyes again to the slender trapeze artist. "Yeah," he muttered, "she always looks good."

"Why don't you go get cleaned up," Dixie suggested. "Then you and I can get Mia, and we can go out somewhere and eat. I've got money saved, and it'd be my treat."

"Why would you do that?"

"Because we're friends."

He looked surprised. But he said, "She wouldn't want to go with me."

"Sure she would, Kirk. She likes you a lot. She really does."

"Even if she did, it wouldn't matter. Her dad thinks I'm no good. He told me to stay away from her."

Dixie shrugged. "If you'd do what that prodigal son did, I bet it'd be all right."

"Yeah, sure," Kirk said bitterly. "And I bet everybody in the congregation thought that Mooey was talking to me. I'm the one that's gone off into the hog pen."

"You don't have to stay there. Jesus changes people!" Dixie said. "Didn't you hear what Mooey said? When the boy went back, his father was glad to see him. I'll bet if you'd just let Jesus change you, then—"

"It's too late for that." Kirk's lips closed in a tight line, and he walked away.

Dixie ran to catch up with him. "Kirk, if you want to change—if you want to win Mia—you'll have to ask God."

"I'm not asking God for anything!"

"Sure, you'll have to!"

"Why would God do anything for me? I never did anything for Him."

"God's already done something for you," Dixie said. "Jesus died for you. He loves you, Kirk, just like He loves everybody else. If you'd just stop running from Him, I'll bet you'd see what He could do."

Kirk stopped and let Dixie talk. He seemed to be more amused now than angry. He even grinned slightly. "You're quite a preacher, Dixie, but I'm in worse shape than that prodigal son."

Dixie took his hand. "No, you're not, Kirk," she said. "Jesus loves you so much."

Kirk looked down with a strange expression in his hazel eyes. Then he walked away.

That afternoon, Dixie took Tater for a walk. When she returned, she tied him outside Helen's trailer and then went inside for a can of root beer.

"I saw you talking to Kirk after the service this morning," Helen said.

"I told him that Jesus loved him. And that I bet he could win Mia if he'd just turn his life over to God."

"You told him *what?*" Helen was astonished. "What did he say?"

"He said he wasn't good enough," Dixie

said calmly. She took a swallow of root beer, then put a Frito chip into her mouth. "But God's going to help him somehow, because I've asked Him to."

Helen leaned back in her chair and studied Dixie. "Does God always answer your prayers?"

"Well, not always as *soon* as I ask Him. And not always the *way* I ask Him to. But I just keep on asking."

"Don't you think that God would get tired of hearing you?"

"Oh, no. God never gets tired of hearing us. He *likes* to hear us pray. My daddy says that He stores up the prayers of His people and they smell good to Him. They're like incense, Daddy says. I've been praying for you too, Miss Helen."

Helen took a deep breath. There was a worried expression on her face. "That's good, Dixie. I appreciate it. I always need prayer."

"Do you like Val a lot?" Dixie asked suddenly.

Helen looked at her strangely. "Why, I guess so."

Dixie thought it was time to take a step further in her matchmaking. "Have you ever thought that maybe you and Mr. Delaney ought to get married and be a family along with Lindsey?"

Apparently Dixie had spoken about something that was very close to Helen Langley's heart, for without hesitating she said, "Val Delaney will never get married again, Dixie."

"But why, Miss Helen?"

"Because of Lindsey. Lindsey," she said slowly, "will never have another woman as her mother—and her father will never marry unless Lindsey changes her mind."

Dixie thought about this for a while, then she leaned over and patted Helen's hand. "I'm going to pray anyhow."

Helen Langley smiled wearily. "That's good, Dixie."

It was clear to Dixie that Helen didn't think anything good could happen. As she left the trailer, she thought, *I guess I'll have to have faith enough for both of us.*

10
TERROR UNDER THE BIG TOP

The summer wore on, and Dixie grew tanned and fit, for she was out in the sun a lot. The cubs took up much of her time, and she and Mickey grew to be fast friends. Eric never stopped tormenting Mickey about playing with dolls. Sometimes it seemed to Dixie that Eric just wanted attention.

"If he doesn't stop teasing me about playing with dolls and cooking and things like that," Mickey said one day, "I'm going to bust him in the eye!"

"Don't do that," Dixie said.

The two were sitting in front of the TV watching an old Shirley Temple movie.

"Why'd you tell me not to hit Eric?"

"Because I think he's really just lonesome."

"He's a pain in the neck! That's what he is!"

"I know, Mickey, but he just doesn't seem to fit anywhere."

"Why can't he fit in with his sister?"

Dixie knew that Eric's shy twin, Marlene, kept to herself much of the time. "She's not company for Eric. He's rambunctious."

Mickey went back to watching the movie. When it ended, he said, "I've got to get back and help with the bulls."

"Why do they call all elephants bulls even if they're female?"

"I don't know." Mickey shrugged. "They just do. I'll see you later. Maybe we can watch something else."

"I'll make us some popcorn."

Dixie cleaned up the trailer. It was so small that everything had to be kept in place. She had long ago learned that she could not leave her Barbie dolls out, but each one had to go into its special compartment. Next she washed the dishes, and when Aunt Sarah came in, she said, "I cleaned up the whole trailer."

"You sure did. It looks great."

"What's the matter? You look worried."

"It's Stripes. He's sick again."

Dixie suddenly remembered that time she had seen someone apparently feeding Stripes in the middle of the night. She told Sarah about it.

Her aunt listened and frowned. "Did you tell Val?"

"Well, no—that was the night the cubs were born, and I was so excited I forgot."

"Stripes gets the same food as the rest of the tigers. If someone's feeding him something to make him sick, I'd like to know about it, and so would Val."

Sarah sat down and ran a hand through her red hair. She was wearing a pair of cutoff jeans and a T-shirt with "Canada" written across the top. She didn't look like a doctor. She looked too young and pretty for that. She also looked tired.

"Val says he may have to get rid of Stripes. He's getting too hard to handle."

"You mean have him killed?"

"Oh, no. They'd put him in a zoo."

"He wouldn't like that."

"He may like it better than what he's doing."

"I think Lindsey is awful, Aunt Sarah."

Sarah looked up. "What's *she* been doing—hurting your feelings?"

"Not mine. Her father's. She wants him to leave the circus, and she nags him about it all the time."

"Well, I can sort of understand that. It's a hard life on a girl, and especially when she hasn't gotten over losing her mother."

"I know, but she can't go around feeling sad all the time."

"That's easy enough to say. Not so easy to do." Then Aunt Sarah said, "In a way, you have more problems than Lindsey. Your parents are so far away. She does have a father with her."

Dixie plumped herself down in Sarah's lap. "And I've got you," she said, "and one day I will be with my parents again."

"That's right, honey. You just keep on praying that God will make that day come, although I'd miss you."

"I'd miss you, too, Aunt Sarah."

The tiger cubs were much more active now and were eating more solid food. The circus had moved to Fort Worth, and as Dixie fed them she was thinking that she'd like to go out and see some of the city.

She glanced up when Kirk came into the menagerie, followed by Val. The two seemed to be having an argument and didn't notice Dixie.

Kirk looked terrible. "You need to get rid of that Stripes," he said. "He's never going to be any good."

Val seemed tired, and Dixie saw that he was angry as well. If he had not been tired and his nerves frayed, perhaps he would never have said what he did. But his eyes sparked, and he snapped, "You're such a quitter, Kirk! You never finish anything you start! You could be anything you wanted to, but look at you! You're nothing but a no-good!"

Dixie wanted to protest, but she knew this was none of her business. She sat quietly with the cubs while the two brothers quarreled.

Finally Val gave Kirk a shove. "Just get out of here! Who needs you?"

After Kirk left, Val turned around and gave Dixie a surprised look. "You here? Sorry you had to hear that."

"I feel sorry for Kirk," Dixie said. She ran her hand over Queenie's smooth fur and said quietly, "He'd be a good man if he just could change his ways."

Val rubbed his chin thoughtfully.

131

"You're a smart girl, Dixie. But how do you do that? I mean, I've done everything I can to help him."

"I know. My daddy always says that people sometimes have to hit bottom before they ask Jesus for help and start back up."

"Well, I think Kirk hit bottom some time ago. I'm worried about him, but I shouldn't have shouted at him like I did. After the show, I'll tell him I'm sorry."

That night following the Grand Parade, Dixie kept looking for Kirk. He came in just about time for the trapeze act to begin. He always came in time to see Mia perform. Dixie went over and stood next to him. "Did your brother tell you he was sorry for yelling at you?"

"Haven't seen him," Kirk said. He was watching the fliers in their brilliant, spangled white costumes test their gear.

Dixie wanted to say something to comfort Kirk, but she did not know how to do it, so she just prayed, *Oh, God, I wish You would help Kirk, even if You have to bring him to the bottom.*

The ringmaster came out and announced, "And now the Flying Marinos! Watch as Mia

Marino performs a double somersault! No other woman has performed this feat in circus history!"

Dixie watched Mia swing back and forth. Things seemed to be going well. But suddenly everything went wrong!

"What's that blasted *truck* doing here?"

A small truck, often used to haul equipment, had started backing up. It was going to hitch onto the cannon that flung the Flying Canzonie through the air, but it was too early for it. "That driver doesn't know what he's doing!" Kirk said with alarm. Then he shouted, "Look out!"

What occurred next happened so quickly that Dixie could hardly believe it. The back of the pickup caught the edge of the net that lay under the trapeze rigging. The driver must have heard the crunch of equipment and panicked. He gunned the truck. But instead of going forward, the pickup leaped backwards and knocked down the poles that supported the safety net.

"The net's down!" Kirk yelled. "Mia, don't do it! There's no net!"

But the crowd was noisy, and Mia's

mind was on the somersault that she was about to perform.

"She can't hear you!" Dixie said. "She's going to try!"

Mia reached the top of her back swing. Dixie knew she had closed everything out of her mind except her father, who was swinging back and forth, waiting for her to come flying through the air. His hands would be there when she came out of the double somersault. Dixie knew that often the difficult stunt did not work and Mia would fall into the net—but now there was no net!

Dimly aware that Kirk had left his place beside her, Dixie stood watching as Mia came down into the final swing. She saw the girl throw herself over the bar of the trapeze and double up. Her body whirled into the double somersault. Dixie was praying that her father would catch her!

"She's not going to make it!" Dixie found herself crying out loud. Mia came out of the spin too late and missed her father's hands. And then she was falling, falling straight toward the hard-packed earth—and there was no net!

Dixie's heart was in her throat. Screams arose from the spectators.

And then, as the girl plunged toward the ground, Kirk ran and stood under the falling girl. He held up his arms and leaned backwards, waiting to catch her. Mia was small, but even her hundred pounds would be a tremendous blow for any man. But Kirk stood there like a statue, arms outstretched.

And then Mia struck him. The force of her weight knocked him backwards. But he caught her and cuddled her against his chest. Then Kirk's body hit the ground, and his head struck the hard earth.

"Kirk!" Dixie ran toward them.

Mia was lying across Kirk's body. She seemed dazed.

"He saved you, Mia! He saved you!" Dixie said.

Mia looked down at Kirk's white face. He was unmoving.

By that time others were there, including Fred Marino, who had slid down a rope and run over to where his daughter was trying to get up.

"Are you all right, Mia?"

"Yes, Papa, but I'm afraid for Kirk."

Mr. Marino hugged his daughter, relief on his face. "I saw him," he whispered. "He ran out of nowhere and caught you. You would have been dead, Mia, if he hadn't broken your fall!"

Dixie saw Mia reach out with a trembling hand and touch Kirk's hair.

"You've got to be all right, Kirk," she whispered. "You've got to!"

11

THE
MATCHMAKER

Dixie and Aunt Sarah and Helen Langley rode to the hospital with Val and Lindsey. Fort Worth was a big place, and it seemed to take a long time.

At the door of the crowded emergency room, Dixie and her aunt watched Helen and Val and Lindsey as they sat on one of the benches inside, waiting for the doctor's report. Val was pale, and his hands were trembling.

Lindsey had been crying—Dixie knew she was very fond of Kirk, despite her harsh words about him from time to time. Helen put her arm around the girl. And then— perhaps because she was upset—Lindsey put her arms around Helen's neck and cried.

After a long time, Helen came out into

the hall. A smile was on her lips. "Kirk's going to be all right," she said. "And Mia hasn't left his side! She stayed right with him even though the doctors wanted her to leave."

"Oh, that's wonderful!" Dixie said. "It's just what I thought God would do."

"What are you talking about?" Helen asked.

"Oh, you know Dixie. She's always matchmaking." Aunt Sarah put an arm around Dixie. "She always thinks she knows exactly what other people ought to do."

"No, I don't either, Aunt Sarah!" Dixie protested. "Just sometimes!"

"Well, you seem to have been right in this case," Helen said. "When Kirk woke up, Mia said she loved him and she was going to stay with him no matter what."

"Do you think it'll make a difference in the way he behaves?" Sarah questioned.

"You know, I think it might. Kirk has felt so discouraged. And sometimes all it takes is one person believing in you to get you going in the right direction."

Dixie was very happy over what she had heard. Now maybe Kirk would let Jesus change him. She waited until she was alone with Helen Langley and said, "My Aunt Sarah says I'm a meddler. Do you think I am, Miss Helen?"

"I think you're a very inquisitive young lady," Helen said tactfully. But she was smiling. "What are you going to meddle in now?"

"Well, I don't call it meddling," Dixie said. "But you know, since I've been with the circus I've seen how much Mr. Delaney needs a wife and Lindsey needs a mother."

Helen said nothing. Then, "Why are you telling me this?"

"I was just watching how Lindsey held onto you when she was so scared about Kirk. It was just like she would hold onto her real mother."

Helen nodded. "That was the first time that she's ever done that."

"You know what I think you ought to do, Miss Helen?"

"What's that?"

Dixie took a deep breath. "I think you need to ask Mr. Delaney to marry you."

Helen gasped. "*What?* Why, I can't do that! It's up to him to ask me!"

"I don't think he's very smart in that way. He's so taken up with tigers and trying to raise Lindsey, he doesn't know what he thinks. But he likes you. I know he does."

Helen shook her head.

Dixie stared at her older friend, thinking how pretty she was and what a great mother she would make for Lindsey. But she saw that Helen would not do what she suggested. She said, "Well, I prayed for Kirk and Mia, and now I'm going to pray for you and Mr. Delaney."

Helen laughed shortly. "That's one prayer I'd like to see answered."

But Dixie Morris was a determined young lady. Once, Aunt Sarah had said, "You are very stubborn, Dixie!"

"No," she had answered. "I'm not stubborn. I'm just *firm.*"

Now Dixie made up her mind. She waited until Val came out of the emergency room, holding Lindsey's hand, and said, "Mr. Delaney, I need to speak to you."

"Well, go ahead, Dixie."

"No, I mean alone."

"Why can't I listen?" Lindsey asked.

"Because it's something between me and your father."

"All right. Lindsey, you run along with Miss Helen. I'll be right there." Val waited until Lindsey was outside, then he said, "Well, is this private enough?"

The waiting room was only half filled now, and Dixie said, "Let's go sit down over there in the corner." When Val was sitting across from her, she said, "Everybody says I'm not able to mind my own business, Mr. Delaney."

"I've noticed that. Though you've been a great help to me, Dixie—with the cubs, I mean."

"I want to help you even more, but I'm a little bit afraid."

Val looked surprised. "Well, you don't have to be afraid of me. We're great friends, aren't we?"

"But I'm going to say something that may make you mad."

"Try me. I don't think I could get mad at anything today. Wasn't that great the way Kirk ran over and just put himself under Mia? He loves her very much."

"He does, and that's what I want to talk to you about."

"About Kirk and Mia?"

"No. About you and Miss Helen."

A strange expression crossed Val Delaney's face. "What about Helen and me?"

"I don't think you know how much she likes you. No, that's not right. She loves you."

Val looked confused. "Dixie, I'm not sure you know what you're talking about."

"I do! I was right about Kirk and Mia, and I'm right about Helen. She really loves you, but she's afraid to say anything to you. After all, it's a man's place to talk first."

Val Delaney stared at her. "I confess to you that I think the world of Helen. But Lindsey isn't interested in having another mother. She hates the circus, and she hates tigers. She hates just about everything."

"She's afraid, Mr. Delaney. She lost her mother, and she's afraid she's going to lose you."

"I can't change my profession. I am what I am, Dixie."

"I know. But if she had a mother, she wouldn't be so afraid. She'd have somebody. Don't you see?"

"Dixie, you don't understand. Lindsey loved her mother so much she would never accept another one."

"Yes, she would," Dixie said firmly. "Didn't you see her when she was scared about Kirk? How she sat in Helen's lap?"

"Yes . . ." Val rubbed his chin. "But I'm not sure—"

"You just watch what I tell you. She needs a mother, and she really likes Helen. She's just afraid to show it."

"Well . . ." He gave Dixie a long look. "I'll think about it, Dixie."

"Good. And pray about it, too."

"You're a little matchmaker, aren't you?" Val said. He reached over and tousled Dixie's hair. "You've made quite a splash in this circus, do you know that?" Then he got up. "No, I couldn't ask Lindsey to accept somebody as her mother that she couldn't really love and look up to. Lindsey is the key."

Dixie was so excited about her talk with Val Delaney that she could hardly sleep that night. She stayed up until almost eleven, and then, when her alarm went off at midnight, she was so groggy she could hardly find the clock to turn it off.

However, she stumbled out of bed and hurriedly dressed. She even decided to take along a supply of chicken livers in her leather purse. Maybe Stripes would be awake and hungry.

When she stepped outside, the air was hot. She had discovered that Texas was hot even at night in the summertime. A breeze was blowing, as it usually did, but it was still hot.

She wound through the maze of trailers and small tents to the cubs. They greeted her, squalling, and crawled all over her after she fed them their formula and performed the caressing ritual. It all took more than an hour.

She loved this time of the night, when it was quiet and she was alone with the cubs. Queenie had become her favorite. Dixie held her in her arms, and the cub licked her chin with its rough tongue. Val had told her that a grown tiger had such a rough tongue that it could draw blood simply by licking.

Then she put the cub down. "I've got to go now, Queenie. I'll see you at six o'clock."

She started for Stripes's cage. Aunt Sarah had scolded her for spending so much of her money on treats for Stripes, but she loved to see him gobble them up.

But when she got to the line of tiger cages, she saw something that startled her.

Lindsey was sitting by Stripes's cage and crying, her hands over her face.

"Lindsey, what's the matter?" Dixie cried, running to her. "What are you doing here?"

Lindsey looked up, and her face was swollen. "I've done a terrible thing, Dixie! I don't know why I did it!"

"What did you do, Lindsey?" Dixie asked. Then her eyes went to the cage, looking for Stripes. The cage door was open. The tiger was gone.

"Lindsey, you let Stripes *loose?*"

"I did! I hated him. I wanted him to go away and never come back, and now he's gone!"

Dixie was suddenly scared. To think about a Siberian tiger being loose was enough to scare anybody.

"Why did you do it?"

"I told you. I've always hated him because his mother killed my mother. And I've been feeding him bad things—old medicine and rotten meat—and I come at night and poke him with a stick and make him mean."

Dixie wanted to yell and scold, but she realized that this was not the time. "We've got to find him, Lindsey!"

"I'll go get Daddy. He'll hate me for this."

"No, wait a minute! Maybe Stripes hasn't gone far."

"Even if he hasn't, we couldn't get him to come back with us."

Dixie Morris looked out into the darkness. Somewhere out there was a five-hundred-pound Siberian tiger capable of killing with one blow of his paw. Then she said, "Let's go find him."

12

A TIGER IN THE DARK

Dixie did not ask God if what she was doing was the right thing to do. She did not ask if what she was doing made good sense. But she *was* praying hard, for she felt very much afraid. It was not an easy thing for a ten-year-old to go out in the dark searching for a tiger!

"Dixie, we don't even know where to look. Stripes could be anywhere!"

Stripes could indeed be anywhere, just waiting for them, Dixie thought. "That's right, Lindsey, but I've got an idea."

"What is it?"

"Come on. Let's go to Miss Helen's trailer."

"You're not going to *tell* on me, are you?"

"Don't worry. It'll be all right."

"She'll hate me," Lindsey whimpered, "and so will Daddy."

"No, they won't hate you, and right now we've got to find Stripes as quick as we can before somebody gets hurt."

Tater was tied, as usual, by Helen Langley's trailer door, and he greeted Dixie with a wagging tail. She reached down and petted him.

"Tater can find Stripes," Dixie whispered.

"What do you mean?"

"*Sh!* He can track anything. Miss Helen used to hunt with him. Well, if he can smell a possum or a coon, he ought to be able to smell a tiger." She unfastened Tater's leash, whispering, "Come on, Tater. It's up to you. You've just *got* to find Stripes."

Dixie led Lindsey and the dog back to the menagerie tent.

There she reached into Stripes's cage for the blanket that the tiger slept on. She rubbed it on Tater's face, saying, "Here, Tater, find Stripes—find Stripes."

The dog seemed to understand what was asked of him. With a whine he began to smell around on the ground while the girls watched him breathlessly. There was already a strong scent of cat in the air, as there always was in the menagerie area, but suddenly, with a fit of barking, Tater ran out of the tent.

"I think he's on the trail!" Dixie cried.

They rushed out behind Tater, who suddenly bayed.

"That's the kind of noise they make when they find the scent of a coon," Dixie said. "He must smell Stripes!"

There were many things to take Tater's mind off the trail, but he kept running back and forth until at last he left the circus grounds and started across the empty parking lot.

"He seems to know where he's going," Dixie said. "Quick! We can't lose him."

Fortunately, the moon was up, which helped them to see where they were going. Dixie could hear Tater baying up ahead. Briefly she wondered what they would do if the hound *did* find the tiger.

She had no time to think long, however. At the end of the parking lot, city buildings began to appear right away. Evidently Stripes had gone toward town.

"If that tiger runs around Fort Worth, anything could happen," Dixie panted. She saw that Lindsey was having trouble keeping up. But they kept stumbling along. And then Dixie said, "Listen to that. Tater sounds different now."

"Maybe he found Stripes."

"We've got to be careful," Dixie said.

Still, how could anybody be careful enough in the middle of the night when there was a tiger loose? Dixie had learned to love Stripes, but suddenly she remembered that he *was* a full-grown Siberian tiger and *not* a good-tempered one at that. Maybe, she thought for the first time, this was not a very smart thing to be doing after all.

The girls slowed down as they approached the sound of the dog's frantic barking.

"There's Tater," Dixie whispered. The dog stood baying next to a big one-story building, looming in the moonlight. "What kind of a building is that?"

"It looks like an old factory," Lindsey said. "But it doesn't look like it's used anymore."

"That's good." Dixie advanced cautiously, ready to turn and flee if an angry tiger appeared—though who could outrun a tiger? "There's an open window!" She pointed. "Maybe Stripes jumped through there."

The window was perhaps six feet off the ground. "That wouldn't be any jump at all for Stripes," she said.

The barking dog was rearing up against the side of the building. He seemed to be saying, "That's him! That's where he is!"

"I'll bet he's in there," Dixie whispered.

"Dixie," Lindsey said softly, "we'd better go get my dad."

"But if he's in there, maybe he'll come back with us and go to his cage."

"No," Lindsey said quickly. "You don't know how bad those tigers are."

"Stripes isn't bad. And anyway, I've got something he likes in this purse. If I can get close to him, he'll come for the chicken livers. He loves them."

"*No!*" Lindsey shivered.

Dixie stood under the window. It was so high she could not reach over it, and she began to feel around in the darkness.

"What are you doing?"

"I'm looking for a box. Something to stand on."

"Dixie, don't go in there! Let's get my father."

"I'm not going inside. I just want to look in—oh, here's an old wooden crate. Help me move it over there."

Lindsey did not want to, but Dixie persuaded her. The two of them tugged at the box, and soon it was right under the window.

Tater tried to jump up, but Dixie said no. "You hold him, Lindsey!"

Lindsey stared up at the window and shivered again. "I just hope Stripes doesn't come out!"

Dixie scrambled up onto the box, and now she could look inside. She could see nothing, however. Except for the dim moonlight at the window, the old factory was absolutely dark.

"Stripes!" she called. "Come here, Stripes!"

"Are you crazy?" Lindsey cried. "Don't call that tiger! He might come!"

But Dixie kept on calling, "Stripes, chicken livers!"

Down below, Lindsey seemed to be having trouble holding Tater. Then she said, "Dixie, I'm going to take Tater back. I'm scared. I'm going to get my dad, Dixie. Dixie?"

Dixie did not answer. She heard Lindsey run off through the darkness, and she heard Tater yelping, but she paid no attention.

The darkness inside the old building was as thick as the inside of a black box, but she felt sure that Stripes was there somewhere. "Stripes, come. Get your chicken livers!"

She was thinking about giving up, when she heard something. It was not a very loud noise. Next, she *saw* something—a pair of green eyes that caught the reflection of the moonlight behind her. Dixie swallowed hard and tried to keep her voice steady. "Come on, Stripes! It's time for your chicken livers!"

And then the shadowy form of the tiger glided up to the window. He looked enormous in the feeble light, and his eyes glowed like green coals.

And Dixie realized how foolish she had been. She prayed, "Oh, God, I shouldn't have done this. But please help me. Help me get him back to his cage." Reaching into the purse, she found a chicken liver and held it out.

"Here, Stripes! Take your liver!" Her voice trembled a little.

And then the enormous head of the Siberian tiger appeared at the window, right across from her.

Stripes opened his mouth. For one moment Dixie was afraid he was going to bite her hand off. But then his tongue came out, and he lapped up the chicken liver. A rumbling came from his throat. It was not an angry sound but, instead, the rumble of pleasure that he always made when she fed him livers.

"Come on, Stripes, come out! Get another liver!" Dixie jumped to the ground.

The great cat gracefully leaped outside and landed on the crate. He dropped to the ground and walked up to Dixie. He was nearly as tall as she was. He nuzzled her hand with his huge head.

Dixie began to feel just a little less afraid. "Sure, Stripes," she said, "you want another liver." She took another from her bag and gave it to him. "Now, come on. You have to come with me. You can have all the livers you want."

It seemed a thousand-mile journey back across the open field and past the trailers. She stopped every once in a while to give Stripes a liver and pat his head. Her heart was still pounding, and she just hoped they didn't meet anybody.

Finally they reached the menagerie, and the other tigers rumbled as they went inside. Dixie went straight into Stripes's cage. He came in with her. She fed him another chicken liver. There weren't many left now. As he ate it and rumbled deep in his throat, she rubbed his head. She fed him another and wondered if he would let her back out when they were all gone.

And then she heard the sweetest sound she thought she'd ever heard.

"Dixie!"

Val Delaney had come into the menagerie tent. His shirt was unbuttoned, his hair was rumpled, and his eyes were wide. Behind him stood Helen and Lindsey, absolutely still, their eyes big with fright.

"Be easy, Dixie," Val whispered.

"All right, Mr. Delaney."

Val approached the cage very slowly.

Dixie kept talking softly to Stripes. She reached into her bag and took out the last of the livers. "Here you are, Stripes. It's a reward for being a good boy."

By this time Val was at the cage door.

"Slow and easy now, Dixie. Don't run."

She patted Stripes on the head and backed out.

As soon as she was outside, Val slammed the door shut. He passed a trembling hand over his forehead. Then he gripped Dixie's shoulder. "Dixie Morris, what you did was very foolish! Worse than that, it was stupid. Don't ever, ever, ever do a thing like that again!" Then, as though suddenly remembering, he asked, "Are you all right?"

"I'm all right, Mr. Delaney! Stripes was very good. I think he's actually glad to be back. I don't think he liked it out in that old factory. But I know that what I did wasn't very smart, and I'm really sorry."

Helen threw her arms around Dixie. "Oh, Dixie, I was so frightened when I heard."

"I'm really all right."

Val Delaney still had a hand on her shoulder. Dixie saw his other arm go around Helen Langley.

Dixie looked over at Lindsey and said, "Come on, Lindsey, you can get in on this, too."

Lindsey came, and Helen opened her arms. Then all four of them stood in one big embrace.

Dixie Morris nodded with satisfaction. *It's going to be all right,* she thought. *Aunt Sarah won't fuss at me for meddling this time!*

13

DOLLS AREN'T SO BAD

Dixie watched with pride as Stripes went through his routine. She was waiting outside the performance cage, wearing a beautiful dress of pure blue silk. As a matter of fact, it was an exact copy of Barbie's favorite dress-up gown. Dolly Stoltz had made it for her. She admired it as the animal trainer in the cage put the tigers through their paces. Finally he spoke to each of them, and one by one they dropped off their perches and ran out—all except one.

Dixie felt a hand on her shoulder, and she looked up at Val. "Time for your act, sweetheart."

"All right, Mr. Delaney."

The ringmaster's voice blared over the loudspeaker. "And now we have a new star under the Big Top. The magnificent Stripes, five hundred pounds of muscle and sheer strength—*and* Miss Dixie Morris, seventy-five pounds of beauty and grace. You will now see beauty and the beast!"

Dixie slipped into the cage through the steel door that Val opened slightly. Kirk Delaney, his eyes clear, was taking his brother's place under the Big Top.

Kirk was by Dixie's side instantly. After a glance toward Mia standing by the cage, smiling at him, he said, "Are you ready to do your thing, Dixie?"

"I sure am."

Kirk returned to the center of the ring. He held the silver baton over his head and called out quietly, "Stripes, down!"

The magnificent Siberian tiger came off his perch in an easy jump and strolled across to where Kirk stood. "Are you ready, Stripes?" He gave a signal, and Stripes nodded, something that Kirk and Val had taught him.

"All right, honey, do it!" Kirk whispered.

Dixie glanced over to where Mia Marino stood, her eyes glowing. In a loud whisper Mia said, "Go on, Dixie. Do it."

Dixie walked up to Stripes, and a hush went over the crowd. The tiger was so large and powerful, and Dixie looked almost like a Barbie doll.

But she was not afraid. First, she reached out and took the tiger by the ears and kissed him. Then, slipping her hand inside a secret pouch, she pulled out a chicken liver and said, "Here you are, baby."

Stripes took the liver and tried to lick her face. Dixie avoided his rough tongue and, moving to one side, hoisted herself up to sit astride the tiger. "Go," she said, and Stripes began to walk around the cage.

It was the only trick that Dixie knew, and all she had to do was hold on. Stripes knew what was to come next. He began to walk faster around the cage as Kirk gave commands. Dixie leaned forward once and said, "Chicken liver," and slipped him a morsel.

Faster and faster Stripes went until, finally, at Kirk's signal he unleashed a mighty roar that could be heard clear outside the Big Top.

The crowd was still holding its breath. But then the tiger slowed down, and Dixie slipped off. She put her arm around the neck of the huge beast and said, "It's time for you to go home now." She pointed to the slot, handed him another liver, and said, "Go!"

Obediently Stripes took the liver, rumbled in his throat, and then left by way of his door.

Helen and Val were watching by the cage, each with an arm around Lindsey. There was a trembling smile on Helen's face. She said to Val, "Well, it appears we'll be leaving the act in good hands while we go on our honeymoon." She turned then to Lindsey. "Will that be all right with you, sweetheart?"

Helen knew that Lindsey had had a rough time. She'd confessed to her father what she had done. He had been properly stern with her. She'd wept and apologized. Then he'd drawn her close and said, "You'll never, never do a thing like that again, I know."

"Never, Daddy."

Now she looked up at Helen, who was waiting anxiously for an answer, and whispered, "Sure, Mom, that'll be fine. When you come back, we'll have a great time."

Dixie bowed to the wildly cheering audience. Then she looked at Mia, who was putting her arms around Kirk, and at Helen, who was embracing both Val and Lindsey. She went over to Aunt Sarah and said, "You see? I wasn't meddling."

"You were meddling." But Aunt Sarah smiled. "In any case, this time it looks like your meddling worked."

When the show was over and all the spectators had gone home, Dixie and Mickey sat in the trailer, watching TV. Aunt Sarah was over at the Sullivans' having a late supper with them.

"I don't like this movie!" Mickey complained. "Nothing but a bunch of rich girls wearing fancy clothes!"

Dixie said, "Well, *I* like it, so you have to watch."

"OK, but after it's over, I want to watch something else."

When the film ended shortly afterward, Dixie said, "I want to show you something."

Scrambling up off the floor, Mickey followed her to the back of the trailer.

"Don't tell me you've got a new Barbie

doll," he moaned. "You must have a hundred of them now."

"No, I don't! I've only got twenty-three!"

"So what is it you want to show me?"

"Dolly's been helping me make some new clothes for them. Well, actually *she* made them, but I told her what I wanted."

Dixie began bringing out the dolls. "Do you know who this is?"

Mickey leaned forward and studied the boy doll. "Why, that looks just like Val Delaney."

"It is. It's the same costume, you see? And who is this?"

Mickey looked closer. "That's Helen. That's the same dress she wore tonight."

"That's right. Now look at these two."

Mickey grinned. "That's Kirk and Mia."

"I got Dolly to fix me some other costumes too, and we're going to dress up all the dolls and play circus."

Mickey shrugged. "Might be fun. Maybe we could make a play elephant and a horse."

"What are you two doing?"

Eric Von Bulow came in.

"Playing dolls! What's it to you?" Mickey said. "Now, bop off, will you?"

Dixie saw an argument starting and quickly said, "Come on in, Eric. Let me show you what we're doing."

Eric sat down. "What's all this?"

"See, we're playing circus, and we've got dolls for all the performers—most of them, anyway."

Eric looked at the dolls. "Have you got a real good-looking one that could be me? I'll name him Eric. How about this one?"

"No, that's Robert."

"Well, he's Eric now."

That might have been the beginning of an argument, but Eric did seem to be getting interested. With circus costumes on the dolls, maybe even *he* found them fascinating.

"Hey, this one's just like Bigg."

"That *is* Bigg. See his clown outfit? Let's pretend to do the Grand Parade. I'll hold Val and Helen. And Mickey, you can hold Kirk and Mia. And Eric, this is your father and mother. See?"

Eric squinted at the two dolls. "All right. I'll hold them. What do we do now?"

Thirty minutes later, Bigg, who also had been at the supper next door, came in with Aunt Sarah. They had been talking, but he broke off and came down the narrow aisle. "What are you guys doing?"

Eric looked up, and he had a big smile on his face. "Playing with dolls."

Bigg gaped at him. "Well, the circus is really going to the dogs! Guys playing with dolls!" But as soon as he saw the clown doll, his eyes lit up. "That looks like me!"

"That *is* you, Bigg. Now sit down. We're halfway through the show. It's time for the clown act to come on. You can do all the clowns."

Afterward, when the others were gone and Dixie was in bed, Aunt Sarah came to pray with her. She stroked Dixie's hair. "Did you have a good day?"

"Sure," Dixie murmured. She pulled her aunt's hair, as she often did. "It was fun."

"I'm still afraid every time you go into the cage with that tiger."

"Nothing's going to happen to me," Dixie said. "You mustn't worry."

"I'll try not to." She paused, then said, "You had a good time with the boys too, didn't you?"

"Yes, I did. But you know what, Aunt Sarah?"

"What?"

"I didn't have a doll like you."

"Well, I'm not actually a performer."

Dixie pulled Sarah's head down and gave her a kiss. "You are to me. You're the most important performer in the whole circus."

Aunt Sarah put her arms around Dixie, and tears came into her eyes. "That's so sweet, but now you'd better go to sleep."

"I guess I better. After all," Dixie said, as she closed her eyes and cuddled Celeste under her arm, "it takes a lot of sleep for us circus stars!"

DIXIE GOES TO CHURCH

Hey, first of May! Tell the butcher to stay away from the bulls! We have some cherry pie for him before doors!"

Dixie stopped feeding Rajah and looked up with astonishment at Bigg, who had popped into the menagerie tent. "I don't understand a word of that! What are you talking about, Bigg?"

Bigg was in his clown outfit. He grinned at her. "You have to learn how to talk circus talk, Dixie. First of May is somebody new to circus work. That's from when they started in the old days, don't you see?"

"Oh. Well, then, what's all that about cherry pie and doors?"

"Well, doors means the crowd's coming in to take their seats. Cherry pie, that just means extra work."

"What was that about a butcher?"

"Somebody that sells hot dogs and sodas." Bigg laughed. "If you'd put down those cubs for a while, maybe you'd learn more about the rest of the circus."

"This is my job," Dixie said firmly.

"And from what Val tells me, you're doing a good job. Got to go."

Dixie finished feeding and massaging the cubs. They growled and chewed on her fingers.

Then she got up and left them, passing by Stripes's cage. Reaching into the pouch at her waist, she pulled out some chicken livers and tossed them to him.

This time he came over at once and put the top of his head against the bars. It had become a habit of his. He seemed to like her.

She scratched the top of his head and fed him more livers. When they were gone, he growled and looked at her with his beautiful green eyes. Dixie whispered, "I wish I could come in the cage and pet you, but Mr. Delaney says I can't do that. Well, I'll be back with some more chicken livers before long."

The next day was Sunday. Dixie put on